INTROUBLE

Carolrhoda Lab™
An imprint of Carolrhoda Books
A division of Lerner Publishing Group, Inc.
241 First Avenue North
Minneapolis, MN 55401 U.S.A.

Website address: www.lernerbooks.com

The images in this book are used with the permission of: © SuperStock.

Main body text set in Janson Text 11/15.
Typeface provided by Linotype AG.

Library of Congress Cataloging-in-Publication Data

Levine, Ellen.
    In trouble / by Ellen Levine.
        p.   cm.
    Summary: In 1950s New York, sixteen-year-old Jamie's life is unsettled since her father returned from serving time in prison for refusing to name people as Communists, when her best friend turns to Jamie for help with an unplanned pregnancy.
    ISBN: 978–0–7613–6558–7 (trade hard cover : alk. paper)
    [1. Pregnancy—Fiction. 2. Family life—New York (State)—Fiction. 3. Rape—Fiction. 4. Abortion—Fiction. 5. New York (State)—History—20th century—Fiction. 6. United States—Politics and government—1953–1961—Fiction.] I. Title.
PZ7.L57833In 2011
[Fic]—dc22   2010051448

Manufactured in the United States of America
1 – SB – 7/15/11

FOR ANNE

MARCH 1956

1.

Run, RUN!
Behind me. A lengthening shadow. I see the shadow's edge.
I duck in a doorway and look back.
HIM!
Smirking.
I try to close my eyes but they will not shut.
Run, RUN!
I have no shadow, only His.
I turn the corner and I run.
Down the alley.
Cross the street.
RUN!
I see my block, I see my building, I'm at my stoop.
But the shadow is there. Waiting.
HIM!
I turn and run!

I sat bolt up. My pajamas were drenched. My eyes ached as if I'd rubbed them all night. It's Saturday. Can hardly get out of bed. Couldn't have made it to school. Head dense with nightmare thickness, the same nightmare I've had before.

This has to stop.

"Hey, Miss Meany," Stevie yelled from the kitchen. "Letter for you on the table. Girlie writing."

"Just leave it there!" The smell of toast was oddly nauseating.

I dressed slowly and walked even more slowly into the living room. Stevie was standing by the table. He reached for the letter and grinned stupidly. "I'm gonna open it at the count of three."

"Don't you dare touch that!"

He grabbed the envelope and waved it in the air.

Are all twelve-year-old brothers a pain in the neck?

"Hey, it's only dumb girlie stuff! Nothing interesting." He pretended to tear it in half, then tossed it back on the table and ran out of the apartment.

It has to be from Elaine. She never puts a return address, but she's the only one who writes me. On envelopes, she dots her *i*'s with round circles and sometimes makes balloon letters. Definitely girlie.

It was a short letter:

Dear Jamie,
PLEASE BURN THIS!!!!!! URGENT!!!!!!!!!!

I can't call from the house because my father watches me and if he sees me on the phone he listens. I HAVE to talk to you. I need a HUGE favor. There's a phone outside the public library here. CE 9-0279. Call me at 11 A.M. Saturday morning if you can!!!!!!!!! I'll wait on Sunday also.

THANKS!!!!!!!!!

xoxoxo Elaine

A year ago, when Elaine moved, we talked once a week on the weekend. But you get involved with other things, suddenly it's Monday, and Mom doesn't like me to stay on the phone during what she calls "homework days."

Now, when something happens—*I will not think about It. I will not remember It. I will NOT*—I cannot tell anybody, not Elaine, not Georgina, who's my closest friend now that Elaine's gone.

Not anybody.

Not ever.

10:59. I'm glad Stevie's gone out. I don't have to whisper on the phone. I've got the whole place to myself.

I dialed and the phone rang once. A breathless Elaine answered, "Jamie?"

"No, Kilroy. What's up?"

"I have to come into the city Friday."

"Great!"

"Jamie, listen. I . . . I've been seeing Neil—"

3

"Neil! Didn't your father drag you all to Long Island to keep you from seeing him?"

"Jamie, please." Elaine speed-talked, and it was confusing. "He's come out a couple of times starting last fall and he's got a '51 Dodge and I've met him and we've driven around and . . . anyway, I've been seeing him."

Her voice cracked. Neil was pressing very hard, she said, even threatening to break up. "He says it's a sign I don't love him if I won't . . ." she hesitated.

"That's disgusting!" The minute I said it I could feel Elaine freezing at the other end of the phone.

"You don't understand," she said in a tight voice. "I *do* love him. Besides, maybe he's right. Next year he'll be a college sophomore and I'll graduate from high school. We'll get married."

I took a deep breath. "He'll only be halfway through college. Why would he want to get married?"

"Because he loves me," she shot back.

"He's taking advantage of you," I said quietly, though I didn't feel the least bit quiet. And that's not even half of what I think about Neil and all the guys in the whole world like him. *Who do they think they are? And who does Neil think he is, messing with my friend!*

I breathed in hard and I listened.

Elaine's voice softened. "Anyway, he's coming home next weekend. Well," she paused, "not exactly home. He has a friend whose parents will be away, and they've

4

got an apartment on the Upper West Side, and I said I'd come in." She stopped for a second. "Jamie, you've got to help me. I need to tell my parents I'm staying with you."

Elaine had never been good at making up stories. It was me who used to be the big liar, but not *to* my parents, just about them. That was about politics. This is Elaine thinking it's Valentine's Day, with a card that has three layers of lace around the heart.

Elaine kept talking. "You've got to call tonight when my parents are home and invite me. You just have to." She was pleading.

I hesitated. "My dad's coming home soon, and of course my mom's been anxious about it. So it's not a good time for you to sleep over."

"Oh no, I won't really be there. Friday night and Saturday night I'll be at—"

"You mean it's a *total* lie? But what happens if your mom calls here?"

"She won't," Elaine said quickly, as if to convince herself.

I ended up agreeing, and we said we'd meet a week from tomorrow for lunch at the Automat. Neil, the creep, is meeting friends that afternoon.

Elaine, sneaking off to be with Neil and lying to her folks. The lying-to-parents part I get, but Neil?

The thought of dating—oh god, nauseating. Scruffy, my black cat with a splash of white on his chest, rubbed against my leg. "You're lucky, kid," I said as I scratched behind his ears. "You have no idea what's going on out there."

And right now I wish I didn't.

2.

Two days since Elaine's letter and now one from Dad. This one had a return address, his prison number. Nothing girlie about that.

Ten months, twenty-two days, thirteen hours since the prison gates closed behind Dad. And now just "See you all next Thursday. Dad." That was the whole thing.

Four days.

Important letters get left on the dining room table to be pored over. Everybody's read this one a gazillion times, not that there's much to read. One lousy sentence everybody's thrilled about. Didn't even say, "Looking forward to seeing you," or maybe even "Hey, Jamie, a hug," or even "*love*, Dad." Hardly worth the three-cent stamp. One lousy sentence.

"Stevie, get the damn phone!" Every time it rings my stomach turns over. When Dad started his prison sentence, I was numb. Let Stevie or Mom answer the phone. Not *moi*. Each ring sounded like an ammo belt going through a machine gun in a World War II movie.

When someone answers, I watch their face—good news, bad news, what? Is it some anonymous voice on the other end of the phone saying, "Peter Morse in a fight with another prisoner, sentenced to ten more years"? Or, "Peter Morse disobeyed guards. Refused to stop political talk. Locked in solitary"? Or, "Peter Morse stabbed in the yard and . . ."?

```
Tight close-up on striped shirt with bull's-eye
on back. Picture fades to black. Camera opens
in a wide shot of the whole prison yard. Tough-
looking men in bunches, leaning against the
wall, a dozen or so walking with buddies, most
smoking, all figuring how to "bust out." Camera
moves in on one convict, alone, squatting by the
wall. Dad. An inmate comes over to ask him a
question, and he stands up. As he turns, you see
the bull's-eye on the back of his shirt.
```

That's the movie I see in my head. And when I get to the bull's-eye, I blink and pull my earlobe three times to erase the picture.

But believe it or not, I go to every prison picture, even if it's playing an hour and a half away in Brooklyn. I don't go with anybody. Not even Stevie. A kid brother who squeezes his pimples without thinking as he's talking to you? No way. Besides, *Riot in Cell Block 11*, which was filmed at a real state prison, is hard enough to see when you're alone. I don't want to worry about what Stevie's thinking.

The weird thing is in *Riot in Cell Block 11* the convicts are fighting for better prison conditions, food without rat doo, an end to overcrowding. Just the kind of political stuff Dad would get involved in. He is, after all, a political prisoner. Contempt of Congress they called his "crime." Dad always said he had contempt *for* Congress and for Senator Joe McCarthy for trying to stomp on people with leftist politics.

"It was a hang-up." Stevie came back into the kitchen and filled his milk glass. "And it's Steven to you."

"Damn it, Steeeven, you finished all the cookies!" I grabbed his hand as he was about to bite into the last Oreo.

"You know what Mom would do if she heard you cursing," he said, pulling away.

"Selfish pig! It'll make your pimples worse."

He stared at me. "You really are mean."

Ever since Dad went away, Mom says I've become grim. Absolutely not. Just realistic. After all, it's four days till Thursday. Anything could happen. Brutal warden, brutal guards, brutal inmates. Anything.

Like going on a date, and you think it's okay because he's a friend of someone you trust . . .

. . . RUN!

But I'm awake. I shook my head violently. "No more!" I blurted.

Stevie looked at me as if I were nuts. Then he shrugged and walked away.

Maybe I am.

3.

"Martha Conway's gone!" Georgina paused after each word and then lifted her milk glass as if it were an exclamation point. "Gone!"

Carol looked puzzled. "Gone where?"

"Gossip. That's what it is," Kay was emphatic.

"Wrong." Georgina said. "I heard Nurse Barclay tell our esteemed principal that Martha most likely wouldn't make it back for graduation. '*It's around her time*,' she said." Georgina paused to let that sink in. "And Mr. Shishkin said, 'Just as well. I don't know if we could allow her to graduate.'"

The chill of an official secret settled over us.

"Figures," Georgina added.

We stared at her, and she sighed, as if talking to a group of elementary school kids. Since Elaine moved,

Georgina's my closest friend. We have the same birthday, but we're not at all alike. She picks up on things most of us never notice.

"Martha started wearing those blousy muumuus. Remember?" she said.

That's what I mean about Georgina. She's smart, but also decent. The day Dad left for prison, miserable Gail Boseman was showing the newspaper article to everyone who walked by in the cafeteria. Georgina smiled at me in the hall. That's something you don't forget.

"I still don't understand," Carol said, somewhat irritably. "What was Nurse Barclay telling Mr. Shishkin?"

Kay's fork was suspended in midair. "You don't mean . . . are you really saying . . . preggers?"

Georgina nodded. "She's disappeared."

"I heard someone talking about Martha's college boyfriend," Kay said, "but if you really mean *that*—that's scary."

"She went all the way," I said and shuddered. I saw our cafeteria table as if at the small end of a telescope. Far, far away. That's where I'd go if I were Martha, far away, a safe place at the small end of a telescope.

Run! I'd tell her.

Martha Conway was a senior, a year ahead of us, but we all knew her. She was a cheerleader, and right away that made her a star. She was pretty, with an A– average and a boyfriend in college. There were always rumors about girls who got in trouble, but never someone like Martha.

"Oh, I get it," Carol said with a hint of disapproval. "*That* kind of trouble."

"For Pete's sake, you sound like Nurse Barclay," Kay said.

It was true. No matter the reason you went to the nurse's office, she disapproved. But period pains, *that* drew a positive response. "Better to get the curse than not," she'd say.

"So you're saying Martha's at one of those places . . . you know . . ." Kay paused, ". . . to give birth and then give it up for adoption?"

Georgina was patient. "That's what I've been trying to explain. It has to be. If she'd done the other thing, she wouldn't have had to go away."

Georgina seemed to know things the rest of us didn't.

"I heard about a girl who jumped from the second floor of her house," Carol said in a remarkably calm voice.

We all, even Georgina, looked shocked.

"Not *suicide*," she said, surprised that we didn't understand. "She was trying to end *the pregnancy*." She emphasized "the pregnancy," as if it made perfect sense. "No way I could go through nine months and then give it away," she added. "I'd keep wondering where he was, how he was."

"She could kill the boy," I said and laughed. There was a dead silence. "You know, the one who . . . who did it to her." They looked at me as if I'd burped out loud at a banquet.

"All I know," Kay said, "is I'd find a way to take a train to my aunt in Arizona. She understands about this stuff. She . . ." Kay lowered her voice, "had an abortion."

A nervous ripple shot around the table. When something's illegal big-time, and you see headlines about cops breaking up "abortion mills," you can't help but hold your breath for a second. It was as if the word *abortion* had a circle of black around it, a dead-of-night feeling.

"I think a lady in my building knows someone," I said quickly, blotting out an image of bleak and dirty rooms.

"Really?" Georgina asked. She lowered her voice and looked around. "Good to know."

At least I think that's what Mom and Aunt Sheila were talking about the other night when they said Mrs. Hanson in 6F knew somebody who "could help."

Georgina leaned into the table. "The thing I don't get is, how dumb can she be, going to her boyfriend's fraternity parties every weekend? You'd think Martha'd know by now what frat boys do on those weekends."

Not only frat boys.

"Hey," Georgina said, "a big brother is useful for something." She paused. "They drink a lot, you know, frat boys. You gotta be careful."

"How?" I said with an anger that surprised me.

Who was I angry at? Martha? Georgina? Carol? Kay? Me?

"Yeah, how?" Kay asked. "How can you be careful?" Kay'd been dating Herbie since junior high. Heavy petting. "Boys can try to get those things in a package, but what are we supposed to do?"

I don't date, so I don't care.

Paul is a friend. A friend, nothing more, absolutely nothing. We both like movies and baseball and that's it. Okay, he's editor of the paper and I'm on it, but that's a work arrangement.

We did go to see *Marty* right after it won the Oscar for best picture. The scene where Marty tried to kiss Clara made a big impression on both of us. When we got to my building, halfway up the stoop Paul kind of smashed into my face and then raced away. But I swear he's not my boyfriend. Absolutely not. I don't want a boyfriend.

"What my sister told me," Carol said, "is that they pull out."

I froze.

Everyone else groaned. "Throw-upsville," Kay said.

"Well, it makes sense, doesn't it? Carol continued. "You remember that film in biology class they made us watch, 'Motile sperm meets egg' and all that stuff?"

"Timing is everything, they say.... But seriously," Georgina said, "her parents must have sent her away."

"My father'd kill me. That's why I'd run away to Arizona," Kay said.

"I'm not sure what my folks would do. Maybe ship me off to my dad's sister in Keokuk." Georgina took another bite of her sandwich.

Carol looked at her. "Where is Keokuk?"

We all laughed.

"Maybe Martha's father has a sister in Keokuk," I said, but by then no one was laughing.

"How about your dad, Jamie?" Kay said. "Would you tell him?"

"Hey, didn't you hear the bell?" Georgina said. "See, there's the caf monitor heading over here."

Times like this I'm thrilled there's a caf monitor... and Georgina.

4.

It's not like we live in one of those huge apartments with a living room you could have a wedding in, or a dining room with a table that can seat twenty, or a kitchen a whole family can walk around in. Nope, that's not us. Our dining room table is at the end of the living room. We can squeeze eight around it if nobody gains even half a pound. And the kitchen, well, three rear ends is one and a half too many. But don't get me wrong, it's home.

So picture us all there.

"What is this," I said, "*Waiting for Godot?*"

But I don't think anybody heard me. Besides, it was a cheap shot. Seven of us are definitely waiting for Dad in the living room, but unlike in the play, Dad'll show up.

Aunt Sheila shook her head. "Not now, Jamie." She turned to Uncle George. "What time is Pete supposed to be here?"

Mom looked up, bewildered. "What's happening?" she said, as if she'd arrived late at a meeting.

"How about *Waiting for Pete*?" I couldn't seem to stop myself. "For Pete's sake, at least everybody in that play talked."

Stevie snickered.

"But who knew what they were talking about?" Uncle Maury said. He was right. I didn't get half of it.

"At least they talked," I persisted.

"He's got to find a job," Mom said.

Uncle George shook his head. "What can Pete do? He only knows how to teach math. And McCarthy labeled him a Communist. Forget teaching, with that label it'll be hard to get a job selling bubble gum."

Uncle George is Dad's brother, so you'd think he'd try to be helpful. "Sometimes he's a real creep," I whispered to Stevie.

"That's helpful, George. Thanks," Mom said, echoing my thoughts.

She'd been going back and forth to the kitchen, mumbling something about coffee. You'd think she was worried somebody might climb in the kitchen window and sneak off with the pot. "Don't take any!" she screamed at Uncle George when he headed for the kitchen. "Leave it for Pete."

Everybody was milling in place. Aunt Sheila was knitting and staring at a blank spot on the wall. She didn't look at the stitches, she didn't look at Uncle

George or Uncle Maury or Grandma or Stevie or Mom or me.

Dad will come through the door any minute.

The key turned in the lock. We all stared at the door-knob. A split second of silence, and then "Pete!" "Dad!" over and over. Mom fell back in her chair, and Dad bent down to kiss the top of her head. Uncle Maury folded his arms across his chest and beamed. Uncle George slapped Dad on the back, and Aunt Sheila began to knit very fast, smiling while tears cleared paths through her face powder. She was looking now at Dad, not the wall. Stevie grabbed Dad around the waist from behind. Grandma came out of the kitchen with a cup of coffee for Dad and a plate of rugaluch. "Apricot," she said to him. His favorite.

Me? I sat there, looking at my dad who looked shorter than I remembered. He turned to me and smiled. A very tired smile. "Hey, kiddo," he mouthed. And I started to cry. I rushed up to him and flung my arms around him. I banged Mom's ear and hit Dad in the neck. They both laughed. I kept on crying.

"You look good," Uncle Maury said to him.

I never knew Uncle Maury to lie. Maybe he knew something about people getting out of prison, what it meant to look good or bad after months of being locked away. It seemed to me there was more grey in Dad's light-brown-almost-blond hair. Was that a slight limp? Is he favoring his right leg? I'm not sure.

Camera pans slowly across the barbed-wired yard and comes to rest on a foot twisted at an oblique angle. Widens to reveal the whole leg. Striped pants torn. Close-up of jagged cut. Cut to close-up of lips parted in agony. Widen. Whole face fills the screen. Eyes squeezed shut.

VOICE OVER:
"Morse, get up!"

Inmate rolls to side and struggles to push up from left knee, right leg extended unnaturally to the side. Two guards walk slowly—very slowly— towards the inmate. They're grinning.

"*Zets zikh*, Pete. Sit down," Grandma said, pointing to the big armchair, Dad's chair, the most comfortable in the living room, the one we call the throne. Although we never talked about it, I don't think anyone's sat in the throne since Dad left. It was almost a game: could you avoid it without looking like you were trying?

Dad in the big chair, feet apart, hands cupping the armrests, back matching the curve of the soft cushion. Normal at last.

Run!

Well, not exactly normal.

5.

I pulled on jeans, put on the blouse I'd meant to iron but never got to, and grabbed a sweater and jacket. It was in the mid-forties, the radio said. I took a cup from Mom's morning coffeepot, scribbled a note about going for a walk, and closed the apartment door as quietly as I could.

Elaine's been in the city now for two days. With Neil. We'd had a bad fight on the phone when I said she should forget about him.

"You just don't understand. You don't know anything about love," she'd snapped.

"Love with a capital *L*?"

When I said that, Elaine swore she could see the sarcasm washing over my face, and she slammed the phone down. Now we were talking again, and again about Neil. But she just doesn't get it. "Look before you leap," that corny phrase, should be look and double look before you trust.

I waited at the Automat and scanned the crowd as dozens of people came through the revolving doors. It was Sunday, and most people weren't eating a quick lunch before going back to the office. They looked cheerful in that don't-show-you're-excited Manhattan way.

At last Elaine came through the doors. She looked at me for a second, then rushed over and gave me a hug. And I remembered how much I'd missed her.

If you didn't know, you might think we were sisters or maybe cousins. Both not too tall, not too short. Average, although Elaine's gained weight since I last saw her. Both of us have average brown hair, average length just below the ears. Nothing different, except mine's curly and Elaine's is straight. Elaine always said she envied my curls, and I wished more than anything for her straight hair, which I knew would be perfect in a close-up when the moon shines a spotlight on you.

"Only in the movies," Elaine says, and for both of us that means *From Here to Eternity* with Burt Lancaster and Deborah Kerr making love on the beach in the moonlight.

We hugged a second time, and suddenly I felt shy but glad we were at the Automat. We've loved this place since we were kids. It's familiar. It's our place. You go up to the cashier lady who sits in a closed booth in the center near the door. You hand her a dollar bill, and she hurls coins into the marble troughs in front of her. These ladies never speak a word, even when you ask a question. It's as if they have a union contract that says all they have to do is toss coins grabbed from a bottomless sack of money, nothing else. Their fingers seem to know nickels from dimes from quarters. They never count out your change, just fling the coins into the gullies in front of them. And it's always right. That was the first job I ever wanted.

No waiters or waitresses to bother you in the Automat. Just put your change in the slots and turn the knob. A little window opens and there sits your food. It's easy.

"Hey, you gained weight," I said. She blushed, and I felt stupid. This is the first thing you say to a friend you haven't seen in a couple of months?

I found a table and motioned her over. "What are you going to do about Neil?"

Elaine sipped her tea. She wouldn't look at me.

"You have to think about it," I insisted.

She seemed distracted.

"Hey, Elaine."

She'd been silently crying.

I stared at her. "You did it!" I practically choked on the words.

In a flash I understood this weekend wasn't the first time for Elaine. "Every time you saw him?" I held my breath. She nodded. "That's months!"

Elaine wasn't loose. That's the word everybody uses for girls who did it. Elaine, my best friend for years. I couldn't stop looking at her. She looked only at her cup.

Why would she do this? How could she? Oh my god. I bit my tongue.

Headache stab like jagged lightning.

Run!

"For months?" I said again. She looked shaken.

Elaine had moved out of the city by the time they showed us the sperm-egg film. Did they teach any of that in parochial school? I mean even if you're a nun, you'd know about that, wouldn't you?

"Was he careful? Elaine, you've got to be careful. If you got . . ." It was unthinkable.

Elaine stared at me.

"You have to figure out a way to be safe."

Elaine's cup rattled loudly in the saucer. Tea spilled on the table. She sat unmoving as it flowed in a stream towards her. I grabbed a batch of napkins and leaned over. "Jeez, Elaine, get a grip on yourself."

She looked at me the way you'd eye a stranger. And I sat back and shut up.

"Neil said you could count the days to make sure it was safe." She looked down at her hands. "But I'm not sure I did it right."

"Do they teach you biology in your school? Like men and women, and—"

"—sin." Her voice was almost a whisper.

My heart began to pound. "Sin?" I said. "What about the science things that happen when you . . . when you do it. Like sperm and egg, that stuff. Did they tell you about that?"

Elaine turned such a flaming red I thought she'd have burn marks for life. It seemed like an hour later she said, "Not really. But Sister Mary Joseph had us write down questions about dating and sin. A lot of us wanted to know if making out was a sin."

Sin was clearly the big word.

"But making out isn't going all the way," I said.

A little necking, that's all. Second base.

Run!

"Sister thought it was. Fornication is a mortal sin, and every day they tell us we shouldn't be 'an occasion of sin.'"

"An *occasion*?" I said, completely puzzled.

"Girls shouldn't tempt boys into committing a sin."

I needed a piece of chocolate cake. When I got back to the table, Elaine had destroyed her napkin. It sat in a pile of twisted little balls.

"If you love someone, how can it be so terrible?" She was almost pleading.

I'm no help. The only thing I know about the Catholic Church is that there are beautiful windows and people light a lot of candles. But I tried. "It's okay if you plan to get married, right?"

"That's what I think," she said, looking up. "It's only out-of-wedlock temporarily."

"How temporary?"

"Next year we'll be married."

Oh god, she really thinks that's going to happen. I started to tear *my* napkin. "Listen," I said, "I don't know how they do it, but boys can get those *things*. Neil must know. He's in college."

Elaine shook her head. "He said it would spoil everything."

I didn't know who was more embarrassed. "Why?" I said, concentrating on my napkin. "I mean how?...I mean..." but I didn't know what I meant.

She bit her lip and sighed. "He says it keeps us apart."

Now I really didn't know what she was talking about, but I wasn't going to ask. Georgina would have understood. Maybe it did help to have a big brother, although when I pictured Stevie as older, the thought of asking him about this was revolting.

"Look, I know you're probably right, but I have to go home," she said, slipping her arm into her jacket.

I reached across the table and patted her hand. That's what adults do, pat your hand when you're upset. But it felt right, and Elaine gave a wan smile.

"Did I ever tell you that my Uncle Maury once worked at the Automat?" That got her attention. "Yup, he was a pie man. Bet you never thought about how all those dishes get behind the little windows."

Elaine glanced at the nearby bank of food windows.

I leaned forward with my revelation. "Lots of workers stand behind them, and as soon as one is empty they rush to refill it."

Elaine smiled.

"But leave it to my Uncle Maury. He flunked pie window!"

Elaine actually laughed. "Why?"

"Put blueberry in where apple was supposed to be."

"And they fired him for that?"

"No, but when he mixed up cherry and mince, that was the end."

"Oooh, not mince!" Elaine laughed again.

"Come on," I said, as I pulled on my sweater. "Let's go."

She stood up as if she were fifty years old with knees creaking and back bent. "Hey, listen," I said, "it'll be okay."

Outside, clouds drifted across the face of the sun. Dark and light, light and dark. We headed for the subway. It's an accident of birth that I'm not Catholic. But if you're not Catholic, is *it* still a sin?

We waited at the Long Island Rail Road station for Elaine's train home. I don't remember when we'd had so many cups of tea.

"There's no bathroom on your train, is there?" I asked.

"No, but you know me, I'm a camel."

We stood there not looking at each other. "You're a junior in high school," I said in a low voice. "You live with your parents. It doesn't make sense to get married right away. You always said you weren't going to be like your mom, all day at home raising a kid—you were going to go to college, be something—we were going to go together."

"Yeah, well things change," Elaine said softly. "They change."

Then she turned and walked to the candy stand. I followed her.

"Boarding Track 19," the loudspeaker blared. We rushed back. A quick hug and Elaine was gone. I watched dozens of people go down the staircase to the track. Backs of all kinds, broad-shouldered, narrow, hunched over, skinny, plump, wearing expensive jackets, baggy sweaters. Two teenage boys and a man with a briefcase were the last to go down before the gate closed. I couldn't see Elaine anymore.

"Final call Track 19. Woodside, Forest Hills, Kew Gardens." The voice recited the names with singsong emphasis, WOODside, FOREST Hills, KEW Gardens." Country names, not my world, not the city. And like Elaine, far away. "LOCUST Manor, ROSEdale, VALLEY Stream . . ." The voice droned on.

"Things change," Elaine had said. And how. Only yesterday we were trading movie star pictures, loving Gregory Peck and Ava Gardner and Jimmy Stewart. I turned away from the gate.

I made my way past the coffee shop and newsstand and headed for the subway turnstile. Do dreams change, or is growing up giving them up?

I hate change.

6.

Nobody was home when I got back. I opened the door to my room and jumped back, startled. Dad was standing next to my bureau. Strange. He never wandered in and out of our rooms. At least he didn't used to.

He waved his hand back and forth as if in explanation. "It's about opening and closing doors with nobody watching," he said. "Who'd have known that would be so satisfying?"

"Everybody out?" I asked. A dumb question, since it was clear Dad and I were alone. In the old days, the days before Dad went away, he would have made a joke about my powers of observation. Today he seemed not to hear.

"Want a cup of tea?" he asked.

I started to say I'd had a lifetime's worth of tea today, but caught myself in time.

"Sure."

His shoulders sagged as he walked into the kitchen. He's definitely shorter. I sat in the living room at the end of the couch farthest from the kitchen. It's crazy to feel nervous about talking to your own father. He came in carrying the tray with a plate of Grandma's rugaluch.

"I ate all the apricot, but the raspberry are almost as good," he said.

This is my dad. He looks mostly like himself, but something's different in his eyes. What has he seen?

First time ever in my whole life I ate rugaluch without pleasure.

Dad wiped away a flake of crust from the corner of his mouth. "I wrote you a letter—at least fifteen drafts."

"Cutting-room floor," I said. Dad and I used to talk about movies a lot. Before.

He nodded. "I want to tell you I know it's been hard." He put the plate down and stared at his hands. When I was little I used to count the freckles on the back of his hands. Took me a while to learn how to say "fifteen." His hands looked paler now. I looked away. I can't stand remembering what used to be.

"I know how much you've helped Mom with everything around the house and with Stevie."

I shrugged, but he went on. "I do know. I know it's been tough." His voice broke.

"It was fine," I said. "Really. Everybody chipped in, and Stevie didn't need too much pushing. Really, I mean it. It was okay."

I didn't say that Mom wasn't around much. In the apartment she'd close her door and work, or go off to the library and work, or visit some publisher's office and work. And even with all that work we still had to be extra careful about money.

"It was okay" I said again. "Besides, you know with Grandma it's always FHB with company." I wanted to sound cheerful, but Dad shook his head ever so slightly. He probably guessed it was Family Hold Back every night. But I plowed on. "And Uncle Maury gave us his Christmas crate of oranges."

"Jamie, Jamie," he said with a sigh. "Christmas comes once a year." He riffled his hair. "I know you thought I could have avoided prison if I gave the Committee names—"

"Listen, Dad, I . . . I think you're the bravest person I know. It would have been easy to tell them what they wanted to hear. I didn't understand at first, but I . . ." —it was hard to say— ". . . I was wrong." Dad ran his fingers through his hair. He started to speak, but I kept on talking. "Anyway, it had to have been tougher for you than us, right?"

"Left."

That's my dad. "You know, I used to hate it when you made us say, 'Is that correct?' But now, now it feels like you're really home." He smiled. "But really," I said, "what was it . . . I mean . . . the other prisoners . . . fights? . . . you know, like in the movies? . . . beatings and stuff . . . ?"

I forced myself to keep looking at him.

Dad came over to my end of the couch. He sighed deeply. "It was a federal minimum-security prison, but can we talk about this another time?"

Walls.

"Yeah, sure."

We sat in silence for a couple of minutes.

"I couldn't write a letter when all I wanted was to put my arms around you and Stevie and Mom and everybody I love."

Then he hugged me for all those lost months, and I felt a drop on my cheek. I think he was crying, but I made myself not look. Everybody has something to cry about, I thought, and stiffened.

Run!

He straightened up, leaned back, and put his hands on my shoulders. "Jamie, what's wrong?"

"Wrong? Nothing's wrong."

Nobody. You tell nobody. Most of all not your father.

APRIL

7.

The *Record* office was empty when I got there early Monday morning. It was only third period, but Paul's in-box was already filled with next week's articles. He's a good editor, but we fight a lot. He says we're news-hounds and have an obligation to expose anything kept under wraps. "Expose" to him means not letting Mr. Shishkin, the principal, get away with saying there are no funds for the after-school art club when there's lots of money in the school budget. I'm okay with a story like that, but after Dad was "exposed" for being a one-time member of the Communist party—what can I say? For me, if you could taste the word "expose," it would make sweet seem sour.

Paul says I have to think past my family. But when the real newspapers printed Dad's name on the front page and said he was fired from his teaching job because of his "alleged Communist Party affiliation," some of Mom and Dad's friends crossed the street when they saw me coming. Crossed the street! Like they could get poisoned from something seeping down the sidewalk cracks.

These days I do a roundup of outside-world stories, which means I have to read real newspapers. My lead this week is Elvis Presley. I didn't know anything about him, but he was on the *Milton Berle Show*, and Kay came in the next day saying nothing in her life would be the same after "Heartbreak Hotel." Kay gets carried away, but when Georgina, always calm, came bopping into the cafeteria singing about heartbreak and living on lonely streets—well, after that I knew Elvis Presley would be in my roundup. Research meant listening to the record, which was not a bad assignment.

"Hey, Jamie. Finished?"

I whipped around. Paul always opens the door so quietly he could be an FBI spook. "Hey, Paul. No."

He was persistent. "When?"

"Thursday."

"That's cutting it too close."

I sighed. "That's me. Living on the edge." What a joke. Except for politics, I'm really conservative. I wear a lipstick called Pale.

"Thursday's not good enough," Paul said. "Everything has to be proofed that day. So it's gotta be Wednesday."

"Yessir," I said.

"That's what I like. Fealty." Paul has a crooked smile that I admit I think is cute.

The best thing about Paul as an editor is that he loves words. He finds new ones every day, like fealty, that he puts on the office blackboard. Today's was OSCITANT: "Some of you have been singularly OSCITANT of late. Wake up!" The dictionary was open to the page: 1. Yawning, gaping from drowsiness. 2. Inattentive, dull, negligent.

"See, no yawning," I said.

Anyway, the last thing in the world I feel right now is inattentive.

"At least give me a rundown of your stories," he said, tapping his pencil on the notebook he always carries.

"You know that boycott of the buses in Montgomery, Alabama?"

"Where the Negroes have to sit in the back."

"Right. Well, it started after a Negro lady wouldn't give up her seat to a white man."

He nodded.

"But guess what? A teenage girl did it before the lady." I watched Paul closely to see if he'd known that. His eyebrows rose—Yes! a sweet editorial coup. I checked my notebook. "Claudette Colvin. She's fifteen, and the court case is in her name and three other people's, *not* the lady." I paused to let that interesting fact sink in. "It's what you always say, Paul. Kids can make a difference."

"Yeah, yeah. No toadying to the boss!"

"And the lead is a piece on Elvis Presley."

"The new singer?"

"You didn't watch the *Milton Berle Show*?" Actually I hadn't either. "Then you'll have to wait to find out."

He nodded. He's good that way. If he trusts you, he's willing to give you a little room to play.

"What happens if I can't make it Wednesday?" I said.

He scowled. "You won't have a byline this week, not something any serious writer wants to forego."

He's right. I like having a byline.

Paul tossed his notebook onto the desk, always a sign he's finished with *Record* business. "Want to listen to the Dodger game this weekend?"

We have a radio in the office, and we're allowed to come in on Saturday to work on the paper. Kay asked me if I was dating Paul. I said absolutely not. Besides, no way a radio date is a date.

"Sure," I said.

"By the way, isn't your dad supposed to be coming home soon?"

Paul's been a good friend through all of this, and I trust him, but I can't help it, it's not something I want to talk about. I grabbed my books and headed for the door. I tossed an answer so very casually over my shoulder. "Yup. He's home. See you later."

"Wait up, Jamie. Another assignment."

I could walk out on friend Paul, but not editor Paul. I remained by the door.

"I'd like an article about what it's like to be a political prisoner in our system."

I froze. "You can't ask me to do that. I'm sorry, you just can't."

"Hey, I'm not crazy. I know that."

I reached for the doorknob.

"*I'd* like to interview him. Will you ask him if he'll do it?"

I stared at him. "You're serious?"

He nodded. "Maybe after the Dodger game we could go back to your apartment."

"I'm going to skip the game." And I left.

8.

Dad had been almost completely silent the first week after our one talk. It was as if he was fighting just to get through each day. He was better, he kept saying, but I wonder if Mom has seen him cry.

For me, it's back to a little bit of normal, like having tea and cookies with Grandma after school if I don't stay late. We were in her room, the tray on her night table, Grandma in her rocker, me on her bed, when the phone rang.

"It's for you," Grandma said.

She handed me the phone. Before I could say a word, I heard Elaine scream, "Jamie! Where are you!" Even Grandma could hear her. She adjusted a hairpin, nodded, and went into the living room. She's good that way.

"I'm here. What's up?" I pictured Elaine twisting the lock of hair behind her right ear. She did that whenever she was anxious and didn't have a napkin to shred.

She talked with an urgency I'd never heard in her voice before.

"It's not regular putting-on-weight," she said. "I . . ." her voice shook, "I think I'm pregnant."

"*Pregnant!*"

"I'm late."

"Are you sure?"

Silence.

"How late?"

She spoke so softly I had to press the phone against my ear. "I've missed it a couple of times."

"A couple of times!"

We've been best friends, but we'd never talked about periods except when we first got it. After that you only said something if you had cramps. Even if you got it at school and needed a pad, you went to the nurse's office. The rest was too . . . I don't know . . . specific.

Her voice sank to a whisper. "Beginning of last year when I had that thyroid thing and my mom took me to the doctor, I'd missed four months in a row. The doctor said I had 'low thyroid'—whatever that is—and the medicine fixed it and I got my period. So this time . . ." now I could *hear* her twisting her hair, ". . . I figured the thyroid thing had come back."

I don't know where the thyroid is, and I didn't ask.

"Well, *I'm* never exact," I said finally. "I can be a week late."

"This is months, Jamie." She started to cry.

Months! I was too afraid to ask how many.

"Well maybe when you, you know, after you . . . well, maybe it changes something. Maybe you get less regular. Maybe . . ." I had no idea what I was talking about. "You said Neil told you about counting days. In the film they showed us, you start counting from the first day of your last period, and two weeks later is when the egg—"

"I don't know and I don't care about eggs! I don't have my period!" She took a deep breath. "And I've been wearing a girdle."

I desperately wanted to hang up.

"What will you do?"

She didn't say anything.

"Elaine, you have to do something before it's too late. You've got to think this through."

"What can I do? My father will kill me. My mother's face is tighter than usual. She's working overtime not to guess."

"Why would she think it?"

"I didn't want to go to the doctor with her, you know, that exam they do to see if something's wrong, and then I know he'd tell her, you know what I mean. So I didn't say anything. I rolled up pads and threw them out a couple of months in a row. She makes me a special tea whenever I get cramps, and this month I forgot to say anything. I forgot everything, cramps, tea, pads, every-thing. And I saw her checking the Kotex box. I think she was counting."

I couldn't decide if counting how many pads were left was nuts or super smart. I pictured Mrs. Reilly's face. Very small. Very sad.

"I think I know somebody who could help," I said.

Elaine coughed.

"I don't know, I don't know," she moaned.

"Well, I do," I said with an authority that surprised me. "And my cousin Lois does." That also surprised me. I haven't talked to Lois in a couple of months and don't want to. But this is an emergency.

We were both silent. "Look, I know you're trying to help," she said, "but it's helpless."

"You mean hopeless? It isn't. I'll call Lois and call you back."

I hung up.

Pregnant!

I wanted to yell, How could you be so stupid! In class they had told us about counting and that it wasn't exact, only a way to try to figure the right time to do it if you wanted a baby, and of course the opposite, when you had to be careful. I know it's ridiculous, but all I could think about was that Elaine was lousy in math.

I dug into my bag for my leather address book with its red cover. I've had it since eighth grade and it's nearly full. I turned to the *L*'s.

Lois. Lois would—must—know what Elaine should do. I dialed and waited through four rings.

"Hi," Lois said.

"Hi," I answered, my voice breaking. "It's Jamie."

"Oh, sweetie, I'm so glad you called. I've been trying to reach you. I don't want to think you're avoiding me, but . . . won't you talk to me? You left so quickly that morning . . . was it something I said? . . . did you get my messages? . . . Jamie, are you still there?"

"Yeah . . . sorry . . . anyway, me and my friend Elaine . . . I think I may have told you about her . . . and . . . well . . . I'd . . . I mean we'd . . . I mean . . . I don't know if you're busy but can we come and see you?" I took a deep breath, "Girl trouble." Weird how that covered everything.

"Hey, kiddo, I'm here. You've got my address."

We agreed we'd see her on Saturday, and I'd call to tell her what time.

I can't believe I made that call.

Run!

9.

The next day in the caf I headed for the table where Kay and Georgina were sitting. Carol was at the back of the line. Everyone usually went around her, for she always asked the hairnet server ladies questions about every dish. She couldn't help herself. "Well," she'd always say when we'd tease her, "don't you want to know what's going down your gullet?" When I looked back, she was hovering over the Jell-O and pudding dishes.

"Why are you all whispering?" Carol said in a loud voice when she arrived.

Georgina rolled her eyes. "Don't you just hate it when people say that, like 'Why are you kicking me under the table?'"

"Sit down, Carol," Kay said. "We weren't whispering. I just asked Jamie if her dad's home like the paper said and if she's heard from Elaine."

"Is he and have you?" Carol asked me.

"Yeah. Elaine's fine," I hesitated, "and my dad is too." Now that's at least one major lie, possibly two. I stood up. Time to cut this short. "Have to check up on my assignment from the *Record* office. See you guys later." Three nods. Last week I was added to the paper's masthead, so everyone accepts that I have additional responsibilities. Right now, though, I need to be alone, to stop feeling so rattled.

Nobody knows about Elaine and everybody knows about Dad. Before he went to prison, I never talked about my family. I made up stories. If you took the elevator to the third floor of our building, there'd be no apartment 3C. I made us invisible to the world.

No more.

The bell rang, and kids started to pour into the hallway. Gail Boseman's locker was near mine. Too near. There's always one in your class who makes you feel like all of you is a huge scab that's been picked at. That's Gail Boseman.

"So, Jamie, I see you're now on the *Record*'s masthead." She held up the latest edition of the paper.

This is when you'd die for a snappy answer.

"I remember in junior high," she went on, "when some kids thought you should have been kept off the school paper."

The sharpness of the pain startled me. Back then I only wrote articles about the Thanksgiving pageant or the new cafeteria menu. Safe stuff. Then, splat, Dad's name was in the *New York Times.* The next day half the school knew who I was, and I was thrown out of the newspaper homeroom. Me, who'd never missed a deadline. I'd fought it and got back on the paper. But Dad didn't get reinstated. The Board of Ed fired him, the best math teacher in South Side High on the other side of the projects. One day in the classroom, the next day gone, then behind bars. And now, searching the want ads. An ex-political prisoner. I haven't talked to Dad about Paul's interview. I want to be there. But I've too many movies-in-my-mind about prison, so I also don't want to be. Dad hasn't talked about it, except to say federal prison is different. Still, you're locked behind bars, in a cell, for months. No exit.

Run!

Suddenly I was angry. For me, for Dad, for everyone in a cell. "Yeah, Gail, and you were one of those kids who wanted me off the paper. Guess you didn't pick the winning side that time."

I turned away and pressed my books hard against my chest until it hurt. I saw Georgina, Carol, and Kay ahead of me, but I didn't hurry to catch up.

10.

I met Elaine at the LIRR information booth at 11:30. As we headed for the subway, I described Lois's apartment in detail. Books on shelves, tables, in stacks. Woodcarvings and framed prints.

Lois was Uncle George's daughter from his first marriage. At the time of the divorce she had run away from home, but I was little and I have no memory of Mrs. #1. Uncle George and Aunt Sheila are all I've ever really known. For over ten years no one knew where Lois was. Then, a couple of years ago, she appeared at Aunt Sheila and Uncle George's door and slept on their couch for a week. She and I had walked and talked and shared many pots of tea. After that she stayed in touch.

I loved Lois, and I knew she was special. Twenty-seven years old and so sophisticated. Knowing all kinds of things. Important stuff. The new exhibits opening at the Museum of Modern Art, the concerts at City Center. She went to readings and lectures at the 92nd Street Y. And she and her friends went to small jazz clubs where everybody smoked, tapped their fingers on the dark wooden tables, drank sophisticated drinks like Manhattans, and ate dripping brie.

Halfway up Lois's stoop I told Elaine about Mrs. Hanson. A backup plan.

"She knows..." I wasn't sure how to say it "... how not to have it."

It was as if the earth opened and the Grand Canyon was between us.

"You don't get it," she said. "I'm Catholic, remember? We don't do that."

"Mrs. Hanson's Catholic."

"Who the hell is Mrs. Hanson?"

It was the first time I'd ever heard Elaine curse.

"She lives in my building. She knows people."

If Lois hadn't opened the door just then, for sure Elaine would have bolted. I managed to get Elaine between me and Lois so I didn't have to give Lois a hug.

The apartment extended from the front hall all the way to a bank of windows at the far end. Lois had an art table down the left side with cans of brushes and pencils and pens. On the right side was a couch that was a foldout bed.

Light streaked through the blinds. I got out of bed, dressed quickly. Run!

If only there was a great eraser for the blackboard in your head.

Elaine stared at the prints that hung on the walls. The scent of cinnamon wafted from the corner kitchen, and a teapot sat in the middle of the table next to a plate of brownies.

Lois went over to the phonograph player and put on a record. A voice like a mellow violin sang "My man, he don't love me."

"Billie Holiday," Lois said. "Nobody like her to nail troubles." She nodded in time to the beat and brought over a basket of fruit.

Was Elaine listening to the lyrics? *Her* man, he don't love her. At least it didn't sound like it. Neil hadn't returned her phone calls, and she'd left five or six messages. Now she sat at the table, hunched over, biting into a yellow apple.

Lois leaned back, tilting on the chair's legs, and rested her head against the wall. I took a brownie, Lois sipped her tea, and Elaine kept her eyes on the rug. Nothing was being revealed.

I couldn't stand the silence. Somebody had to say something. "It's . . . it's . . . this problem." I reached for a tissue from a box Lois had on the table. Did she always keep it there, or did she figure we'd need it? Lois looked at me carefully. I turned to Elaine. "Come on, tell her. She can help." But Elaine wouldn't take her eyes off the rug.

"She thinks she's pregnant," I said.

Elaine shifted in her chair.

Lois sat up. "That's not good," she said. She looked closely at Elaine. "How far on?"

"I'm late," was all Elaine said. She put the half-eaten apple on the table, and she began talking as if she was alone in the room. "He said if I'd do it, it meant I loved him." She was almost pleading. "I *do* love him!"

Lois carried the teapot into the living room. "It's more comfortable in here."

I got up right away, but Elaine didn't move. She stared at the apple. "I didn't tell Father Reynolds in confession. I couldn't say it."

Lois said in a calm voice, "Why don't you come in here?"

I tapped Elaine on the shoulder and pointed to the living room. "See, I told you she'd be able to help."

Lois poured more tea. "Here's what I think. I've a couple of friends who I know will talk with you. I'll check out a good time for them, and you let me know when you can come in again."

Lois looked at me, I looked at Elaine, and Elaine looked at her watch. "I have to take the 2:47 train," she said. "I have to go right now." She got up quickly and went to the door.

I followed. Elaine was halfway down the stairs. "I'm sorry," I said, turning to Lois. "She's . . ."

"Not to worry."

Elaine was at the bottom of the stoop when I caught up with her. "I'll call and find out when we can meet Lois's friends" I said.

She wouldn't look at me.

"Come on, Elaine. She's going to all that trouble to get you information—"

"I didn't ask her. You did."

"But they know things. Stuff we don't—"

"Maybe I don't want to know."

11.

On Monday I left school right at the closing bell. I wasn't up for anything. Not Paul asking about my article, not Kay or Georgina or Carol. Not even Grandma, who would ask me how the day went. I walked past our stoop and headed for the playground benches. Only mothers with little kids would be there. Nobody I had to talk to.

Elaine's problem had given me a way to talk to Lois without being alone together. I sat down and opened a notebook to make a list. It's safe inside a list. Number 1 – Elaine. How could she not want to know a way out? Elaine with a baby! It was unthinkable. In a few years she'd become her mother, pinched face, and who knows, if she had a daughter, maybe she'd end up counting Kotex pads.

I started to draw the woman sitting on a bench across from me. A good half of my pad was filled with sketches

I'd done on the subway. People didn't seem to mind a kid across the way drawing, and I've gotten fast. With a few quick strokes, I get the body angle.

The lady held a book in one hand and rocked a baby carriage with the other. A little kid in the sandbox between us was dumping sand into a pail and then pouring it over his head. He began to whimper, and within seconds he was sobbing. "Eye!" he shrieked. "Ma, it hurts," he wailed. "MAAAAAA! EYE! MAAAAAAA! HURTS!"

"Henry," she said calmly, or numbly, "put down the pail and come here." She cleaned his face and hair with a towel and then poured water from a thermos and wiped his eyes. He sat on her lap, hiccupping. When she whispered something in his ear, he ran back into the sandbox, chirping.

That's what I want. Someone who makes me chirp.

I sketched Mrs. Eye-wiper quickly, and it wasn't bad.

"When does your mother get home?"

My hand slipped at the unexpected question, and a dark pencil line zigzagged across the page. I looked up into Mrs. Hanson's eyes.

I've known Mrs. Hanson for as long as I can remember. She lives three floors above us and is my parents' elevator friend. When I was little, if Mom and Dad had to go out, Mrs. Hanson was my babysitter. I like her. She leaves you alone. You will never drown in a conversation with Mrs. Hanson. Elaine says she's grim, and I can see that. I'd swear Mrs. Hanson was born with her grey hair pinned in a roll like a highway tunnel that travels from behind one ear, up over her forehead, and down below the other ear. It was chilly, and Mrs. Hanson had on a wool sweater. She drew it tight around her and waited for my answer.

"Mom's usually home by five-thirty, quarter of six. Can I give her a message?"

Her lips, naturally thin, vanished as she tightened them. "No," she said and turned to leave. "I'll catch her later."

"Mrs. Hanson, can I ask you a question?"

Holy moly! What do I say now?

She stood in front of me, waiting. I moved my books, which were piled next to me on the bench, and put them down by my feet. Buying time? You bet. But Mrs. Hanson's feet were planted firmly in front of me. I motioned to the now-empty bench space, and with a little cloud puff of a sigh, she sat down.

"Nice day, huh?"

She looked annoyed, and I didn't blame her.

I started talking to the sandbox. "A girl I know got in trouble . . ." I heard Mrs. Hanson fold the sides of her skirt up over her lap, like closing a coat. She waited, but I'd run out of courage.

"Does your mother know?" Her voice was flat. I shook my head and turned to look at her. I'd never noticed how piercing Mrs. Hanson's eyes could be.

She thinks it's me! Do I look like that kind of girl? Mrs. Hanson of all people must know what "that kind of girl" looks like.

"My mom doesn't know her," I said, barely croaking out the words. "Actually, I don't know her well. She's a friend of a friend." A lie. "She has a college boyfriend." The truth.

Mrs. Hanson's hands tightened on her knees. "College boyfriends," she said with distaste. She looked at me like she was calculating something, deciding what to believe. She gave a quick nod, opened her purse, and took out a handkerchief.

"My mom doesn't know," I repeated.

Mrs. Hanson blew her nose and put the handkerchief back in her bag. I didn't look at her face, but I was paying close attention.

"Talk to your mother." Her purse snapped shut with the finality of a period at the end of a sentence. Mrs. Hanson had hands that had washed a lot of dishes. Dry and rough, the nails clipped short and unpainted. She stood up and headed out of the playground.

I don't want to talk to Mom right now. She's busy, and you never know if she's really listening. So you keep on talking, and pretty soon you've told her what you never meant to. I couldn't tell her about Elaine. I'd promised. Elaine was my best friend when all the stuff with Dad happened, and I wasn't going to spill her secret. Not if I absolutely didn't have to. And for sure I wasn't going to tell Mom about . . . anything else. It was a long walk home.

Mom looked like she'd been sitting on the couch waiting to pounce the minute I walked in the door. "So

I saw Mrs. Hanson in the lobby and she asked me every which way from Sunday how you're doing?"

I can't believe how nothing in this family is private.

"She said she saw you at the playground and you seemed distracted."

"Mrs. Hanson said 'distracted'?" I picked at a thread from my sleeve cuff. Sounds like a Mom word, not Mrs. Hanson's.

"Jamie." The tone around my name was dark.

"I have to put my books away," I said, turning toward my room.

"Sit down."

I put my books on the table and sat on the couch. Scruffy jumped onto my lap.

"Well?"

"Okay," I said, staring at the pattern in the rug. I could picture Mom leaning back, folding her arms across her chest, waiting. When I looked up, she was leaning and waiting, arms folded.

"There's this girl in school who's got the gym locker next to me. A couple of days in a row we were in the girls' room at the same time, and—" I paused "she was throwing up."

I caught Mom's eye. She leaned forward.

"The girl was washing her face and crying, so I said I knew someone who might be able to help if she was in trouble."

"Jamie," Mom's voice suddenly went soft. "Are you . . . are you involved . . . you know what I mean . . . with a boy?"

I stared at her.

"I mean it, Mom. It's a girl I know."

She sighed and went into the kitchen.

I could hear the coffeepot rattling as she scooped tablespoons of grounds into the basket. She came back and sat in a chair by the table. She began to wipe the tablecloth, as if crumbs, invisible to the naked eye, were lurking.

"I heard you and Aunt Sheila talking about Mrs. Hanson helping somebody, so I thought—"

"Jamie, you're a young woman now," she said. "I want you to talk to me when you . . ."

I didn't know where to look.

". . . become intimate with a boy."

I must have turned scarlet, because Mom said, "I'm not rushing you, but when the time comes, I'll make an appointment with the doctor."

"I don't need a doctor. There's nothing wrong with me."

"Sweetheart, this is serious. You don't want . . ." she gestured with her hand, "what happened to your friend."

I think I'll become a nun. Scruffy left, and I picked up my books, but Mom wasn't finished.

"Has your friend talked to her parents?"

I pictured Mrs. Reilly wringing her hands and Mr. Reilly charging around their house, waving his newspaper, hollering at Elaine and Mrs. Reilly and the furniture.

"No way that would work."

And no way could I tell her it's Elaine. A promise is a promise.

"This girl's really scared, and I thought maybe you'd know somebody who could help. She says her father will kill her and her mother's counting Kotex."

I didn't know whether to laugh or cry. Mrs. Reilly locked in the bathroom with Elaine, waving a Kotex box, and Mr. Reilly outside, pounding on the door. Then I got angry at Mom because I couldn't tell her. About anything.

"You wouldn't understand," I said. "Not everyone wants to talk to their mother."

He lifted my sweater and unhooked my bra . . .
Run!

Grandma came out of her bedroom, took one look at me and glanced quickly at Mom. "What's wrong?"

"Later," Mom said.

Grandma poked at hairpins on both sides of her bun. She's lived with us my whole life, and I can read her pokes. The number of times equals how serious she thinks something is. Right now, only three.

12.

"Later" meant Mom, Grandma, Dad, and who knows, maybe Uncle Maury, and why not Aunt Sheila and Uncle George—for Pete's sake. Pretty soon the whole world would be talking about "Jamie's friend who got in trouble."

I opened my trig book, but I couldn't get into the world of sine and cosine. Elaine, the hypotenuse; me, one arm; Mom, the other. A heck of a messy triangle. Terrible pun. I closed the book.

I started to pace in the small space between the bureau, the bed, and desk. On and off the rug, in front of the desk, around the chair.

"Hey, didn't you hear me?" Stevie stood in the doorway, his hands on his hips.

"What are you talking about?"

"I've been yelling for the last five minutes. Would you keep it down! You're scraping the floor real loud," he said as if talking to a moron.

I looked down at my shoes.

"The taps, Jamie, the taps. Come on, give me a break. I got a test tomorrow."

"Sorry," I said. But I guess he didn't believe me, because he clapped his hands under my nose. It was like an alarm going off in your face. "Hey, cut it out!" I swatted at him, but he darted away.

I grabbed my turtle bank and spilled the coins on the bed. When I pushed the quarters, dimes, and nickels into the center of the quilt, I decided it was probably enough. There was no way I'd ask Stevie to borrow money.

I tiptoed down the hall, past the bathroom, past the living room. Mom was in the kitchen with Grandma, who was heating water for tea. They were talking in low voices. I had no idea what Grandma would say. What would they all say? Mom and Aunt Sheila at least knew someone who could help. But would they want to help if they didn't know the girl?

The only one I could count on was Lois. I opened the front door. "See you later," and I ran for the staircase next to the elevator before anyone could call me back.

I headed for the phone booth across from the public library. *Lois can help. Lois can help.* The words went round and round in my head. Three words, three steps, and with each step, the thought became stronger, the phone booth closer. I turned the corner and saw the library. "Lois will help," I said to no one in particular.

And she did.

Then I dialed Elaine. My life by the phone, the title of my autobiography. *Be There, Be There, Be There*—the rhythm of the words combined with each ring of the distant phone. I send out pleas to the universe in threes. It's my lucky number. I was born on the third day of the third month in the third year of my parents' marriage, and my arrival made us a family of three.

Elaine, Be there. The last thing I wanted was for Mrs. Reilly to pick up. Mr. Reilly, I knew, wasn't home from work yet. I was safe on that score. "Be there, Elaine," this time out loud. She had to be home to hear the news Lois had told me.

"Hullo." Dull grey came plodding through the telephone wires.

"Elaine!" I sank into the seat, "it's me!"

Silence.

"It's me, Jamie."

Silence.

"Elaine, listen, don't be depressed. I told you we'd take care of this. I just got off the phone with Lois, and any time this weekend a couple of her friends said they'd talk to us."

Silence.

"Hey, Elaine, remember me? Your friend forever? Me, who traded you Ava Gardner for Gregory Peck? Meeeeeeeeeeee!"

"You don't have to yell," she said.

"Did you get what I said? We can get help from Lois's friends."

Silence.

"You know it's not easy trying to help you."

Silence.

"Okay, here's the deal. I'll meet you at Penn Station Sunday morning. Same time, same place, okay?" I kept on talking because I wasn't going to wait through another silence. "Speak to me, Elaine. I'm boring myself telling myself what I already know. You know what I mean?"

Silence.

Long pause. "I'm done. Talk to me or I'm hanging up."

There was a sigh at the other end of the phone. "I can't meet you," Elaine said. "My dad found out I went into Manhattan, and he made me promise I wouldn't do that again without asking permission. My mom looks at me without saying a word. She's wringing her hands a lot, so I'm staying close to home."

"That's nuts," I burst out. "The longer you wait, the more impossible the whole thing is. You won't be able to hide it, and then what do you think will happen? If your dad's angry now—"

"You don't need to tell me that! You think I don't know?"

She slammed down the phone.

Brother, did I ever mess that up. I pulled open the phone booth door and crossed the street. The library was still open. Absolutely anything I could find on any shelf would be better than thinking about Elaine. This was truly dumb. What am I going to tell Lois? I went back out to the phone booth and emptied all the change I had left on the little shelf. There's absolutely no way I can say Elaine doesn't want to come. *I'd* feel too stupid.

The phone rang only once. "Hey, Lois, it's me again. Listen, Elaine and her parents are going away for a short trip, so how about if I come in and get the information for her?"

Lois had said she'd have two friends over, so I knew we wouldn't be alone. Additional insurance: "But I've got to get right back, so I can't stay long." I gave a hoarse laugh. "Think of me like Sgt. Joe Friday on *Dragnet*—just the facts, Ma'am. I'm only coming for the facts."

I could hear her smile as I hung up.

Run!

13.

Focus, Jamie. I snapped my fingers as I walked home. Four days till Saturday. By then I'll have figured out how to make Elaine's story so heart-wrenching Lois won't think to talk about anything else.

So, what would Elaine want to know, or at least what do I think she should know? That got me nowhere. Elaine didn't want to know anything.

I'd have to make her understand. That's what friends do.

Kids were climbing the bars of the jungle gym as I passed the playground. A century ago, when I was a kid, I loved swinging upside down on the middle bar. I was going to be a trapeze star with the circus. "Just wait," I said under my breath to those kids. "You're like Scruffy. You have no idea about the world outside. Ain't no grownups to watch over you when you move out of the playground."

"Ah, talking to herself. A chip . . ." I whirled around as Dad lifted his newspaper from his lap and tapped his head, ". . . off the old block!"

"What are you doing here?" I said.

"I could ask the same."

"I didn't know you liked to hang out in the playground."

"I confess a fondness that lasted until you and Stevie gave up swings. Thought I'd try it again." He patted the bench. "Sit down, kiddo."

There was definitely more grey in Dad's hair. He caught me staring. "What?" he said.

I touched my own hair.

"Think of grey," he said with a smile, "as a sign of wisdom."

"Yeah, sure." I grinned.

"Actually," his voice became quiet, "I earned every one of these."

I pictured the prison yard. "Was it . . . did the other—"

"No luck today with Sealy paints," he said.

"I meant . . ."

"I know. But today was Sealy." His shoulders sagged.

I'd forgotten he had a job interview that morning. "What do they know?" I said in what I thought was a casual voice.

"Oh, Jamie." He put his arm around me. "Quite a lot about paints, and I confess I know nothing. They weren't wrong."

"I bet you could sell anything. Last year I heard a radio program about this guy Dale Cornell who'd just died. He wrote a bestselling book about making friends and getting people to do what you want."

"Carnegie's his name, and it's *How to Win Friends and Influence People*." Dad's tone said "you should have known that."

Grey hair hadn't changed a thing. He always had to correct. "The point," I said, "is anybody can sell anything." I fiddled with a sweater button. "Anyway, I've got to go."

Dad looked up. "I'm sorry Jamie. Stay a bit. An old habit."

"Yeah, I know. Bet the inmates didn't like it."

He winced, and I felt rotten.

"Let's start again. What brings you through the playground today?" he said.

I took a breath. He would find out later, so why not now? "I've got a girlfriend who's . . . who's in trouble." I glanced at him to see if he understood.

"What kind of trouble?" I must have looked uncomfortable, because after a moment he said, "I see. That kind."

I nodded.

"And you're trying to help her?"

I nodded again. "She's a friend."

A raised eyebrow.

This had to be a sore point with Dad. He'd lost I don't know how many friends after his name was in the paper. And it was a so-called friend who'd told Senator

McCarthy's committee that Dad was a Communist. Did he even trust the idea of friendship anymore?

With a renewed firmness he said, "That's what people, what friends do for each other."

We sat without talking. Elaine couldn't have this kind of talk with her parents. She's too terrified to tell them what's happened.

Who am I kidding? *This kind of talk?* One that skips and skirts and avoids?

"Okay, you won't talk to me, but how about my friend Paul? You know, the editor of the *Record*, our school paper." I was enjoying the sharpness in my voice that even I could hear. "He'd like to interview you about being a political prisoner. Will you talk to him?"

Dad stared at me, blinked, and looked away.

"Well, think about it."

I rubbed my left eye hard. It was twitching again. What a mess. Anger seeped out of me like a deflating balloon. I'm going after Dad, but look at me. I haven't talked to anyone, not anyone.

"Listen, Dad, gotta go. I'll see you back at the house."

Baumgarten's Bakery. That's what I need, a jelly donut.

14.

You know how a song gets stuck in your head? This time it was "Hail! Hail! the gang's all here, what the heck do we care, what the heck do we care!" The problem is, in this family everybody cares. They jump in even when you don't want them to. You'd think if they really cared, they'd leave you alone.

There they were, assembled in the living room. In the time it takes to eat a jelly donut, Dad had beaten me home. Uncle Maury and Uncle George had divided the paper between them, Mom was reading *The New Yorker*, Grandma was shelling peas, and Dad was dozing in the big chair. Aunt Sheila sat on the couch, knitting a scarf that filled up a large shopping bag at her feet.

"Hey Aunt Sheila, it looks long enough to wrap a mummy."

And that's how I said hello to one and all.

"Always the joking," Grandma scolded, but she looked more anxious than angry. She was poking hairpins.

"Tuna casserole," Mom said, and I was sorry about that donut. It's not the tuna, but the crunched potato chips on the top that I love. Stevie was setting the table and making a mess of folding the napkins. I followed him, refolding.

"Back off! Can't you ever leave anything alone?" he demanded.

"Big sisters, a pain in the you-know-what!" Uncle Maury said. He nodded toward the kitchen. "Your mother. When we were kids, always on my case."

I glanced at Dad. Guess I'm a chip off both blocks.

"But, Stevie," Uncle Maury added, "this is important: soon you'll be taller."

"Alright, what's this about a friend in trouble?" That's Uncle George. He likes to sound efficient.

"Let's sit down first." Mom came in with the casserole dish and set it in the center of the table on a hot plate.

This is how my family would have run the Spanish Inquisition—torture by interrogation over food. No one in this family seems troubled that a piercing question or pained answer can be interrupted by "who's got the salt?"

"Well," Mom said, "dig in."

Stevie lunged forward and filled his plate. "Can I take this to my room? This is all kinda weird, and I've got a test tomorrow."

Mom looked at Dad, but although he was sitting in his usual seat, he was off on a distant journey. "Pete," she said, trying to bring him back.

He blinked a couple of times. "Fine," he said quietly.

Stevie bolted.

This wasn't going to be pretty. It started like this:

Mom: How far along is your friend?

Me: I'm not sure. She's late. Maybe months.

Mom, *eyebrow raised*: It's important how long.

Grandma: And her mother, she knows?

Why does everyone always ask about the mother?

Me: She hasn't told her, but she thinks her mom has figured it out. (I left out the part about the Kotex box, what with Dad and Uncle Maury and Uncle George sitting there. They don't need to know everything.)

Aunt Sheila: And the boy? Does she know who he is?

Me: For Pete's sake, Aunt Sheila, it's her boyfriend.

I must have been adopted. I couldn't belong to this family by blood.

Grandma: Don't get excited. Could be somebody attacked her. All these apartments, all these people, coming and going.

And it went on. Uncle Maury said, "Once they know, will her parents support her?"

"She's Catholic, and she said Catholics don't believe in . . . well, you know what I mean."

Aunt Sheila coughed. "That is one of those odd

things, seeing as how Catholics have as many abortions as anyone else."

Everyone stopped to look at her, resulting in a blissful, but only temporary, silence.

"People spend an inordinate amount of time believing something they often don't act on," Dad said. Everyone looked at him.

"Welcome back," Mom said quietly, with a just a hint of sarcasm he didn't seem to hear.

Uncle George tilted back his chair as if to launch into a sermon, but Uncle Maury jumped in. "Force of habit for a lot of people. What you grow up believing more often than not stays with you even if it doesn't make sense to you anymore."

Grandma gave three sharp pokes. "Better you should not believe in so many rules. Pick the important and keep to."

When she was excited, Grandma's English could be fractured. Once you caught on, though, she made a lot of sense.

"Nonsense," Mom said. "This isn't theoretical. This is a young girl who's in trouble. The question, it seems to me, comes down to what she wants."

"What if she doesn't know what she wants?" I said. "Maybe sometimes someone has to tell you." It was so clear. I had to make Elaine see. "I mean, Ma, you tell me lots of times what I should do," I added lamely.

Mom shook her head. "I'm talking about big things, life decisions."

"Isn't that just when a young person needs someone to talk to?" Aunt Sheila reentered. "Sometimes help helps," she added.

I giggled. Uncle Maury clapped. Aunt Sheila blushed and ripped out several rows of the scarf.

"If you had children you'd understand," Mom snapped.

You couldn't miss Aunt Sheila's stricken face.

"Sheila, I am so sorry." Mom reached over, but Aunt Sheila pulled back. "All I mean," Mom said, "is that you have to let young people make the decisions important to their lives. We're not talking about a child. This is Jamie's classmate. She's a young woman."

Aunt Sheila's voice was low but distinct. "And I'm saying it's hard for anyone any age to make certain decisions, and if you're young, you've simply got less information."

That was the longest speech I've heard Aunt Sheila make at one of these family inquisitions. She talks at length with Mom about all kinds of things, but in these free-for-alls she's usually quiet.

"Forget my friend for a minute," I said, trying to sound theoretical. "What if you know somebody is going to make a really bad mistake?"

Uncle Maury tossed his napkin on the table. "In the first place, this is not abstract. This is about your friend. And come on, Rachel," he said to Mom, "who are you kidding? You'd fight like a ferocious mother hen to keep your chick in the fold. If Jamie suddenly decided she didn't want to go to college, why, you'd truss her up and haul her off to some freshman orientation before she knew what was happening. This is Jamie's friend."

He patted my shoulder. "What is the nature of your involvement?"

"Involvement?"

Uncle Maury shook my shoulder gently. "Wasn't that what you asked? If a good friend is about to make a really bad mistake, do you have a responsibility—"

Aunt Sheila cut him off. "You can't make someone else's decisions for them. All you can do is give information if they're willing to hear it." She wrapped the scarf around the needles. "And let them know you're there if they need you."

Grandma poked four times. I'm hoping four's all the hairpins she has. I can't take much more.

After Aunt Sheila's pronouncement, it petered out. Dad came back to the world of the living. He and Mom did the dishes while I cleared the table. Their voices were low, but Mom's tone was normal, not edgy like before.

Dad came out to the dining room with a dish towel in his hands. I'd moved all the dirty glasses down to the end of the table. He lifted one and held it up to the light. "Lipstick does leave its mark." He put it back down and looked at me. "Okay about your friend Paul." Then he went back into the kitchen with the marked glass.

Okay to talk to Paul, but not me. Everything leaves a mark, I wanted to yell.

Run!

Uncle Maury left to go upstairs to his apartment, and Grandma kissed me goodnight and went into her room. When Uncle George went into the kitchen to say goodbye to Mom and Dad, Aunt Sheila said, "Jamie, stop by after school tomorrow."

That was a surprise. Usually I go over to Aunt Sheila's when Mom sends me on an errand. "Do you want me to bring something?" I asked.

She smiled in a gentle way. "Just yourself."

15.

I rang Aunt Sheila's doorbell at 3:43. When something changes completely what you thought you knew, you replay it over and over. That's why I know it was exactly 3:43.

"Door's open," I heard Aunt Sheila call. "I'm in the bedroom." I made my way down the hall and studied the framed Van Gogh prints I'd seen a hundred times. The bridge, the flowers. Everybody talked about the famous sunflowers, but to me they were brown and looked dead. I stopped in front of them. The brown hadn't brightened.

"Jamie?"

"Yup, coming."

Aunt Sheila was hanging up Uncle George's pants when I walked in. She took a shirt of his off the chair where it looked like it had been tossed and sat down. Her sewing box was on the radiator under the window, and she picked up a skirt folded on the top. I sat in a chair across from her.

"I'm not in the habit of butting into things," she said.

Aunt Sheila didn't usually plunge directly to the point. She couldn't have guessed. Could she?

"You sound like Uncle George," I said with a nervous laugh. "Did I do something wrong?"

"Oh no, sweetie. It's just something I feel strongly about." Then her voice faltered. She took out a seam-ripper from the sewing box. "I'm redoing this skirt hem," she said, as if by way of apology.

"Would you like a glass of seltzer?" she asked abruptly. "Sure."

She put down the skirt, and I followed her into the kitchen. Glasses in hand, we walked to the living room and sat at the ends of the couch. She took two coasters from a painted wooden container on the coffee table. We bracketed the couch, and the two glasses were like candle-sticks waiting to be lit.

"I like needlework," she gestured with her hands. "It's hard to talk without something to work on."

Why was my own aunt so nervous in front of me?

"It was before the war, before I met your Uncle George," she began. "I'd been on a trip back home to Chicago, and . . ." there was a long pause ". . . well, the details don't matter. Two months after I returned to New York, I went to a doctor." She got up and put her glass down on the dining room table. "He confirmed my fear," she said, turning to me. I must have looked startled, for she added, "It's more common than you might think." She came back and sat down. "Everybody talks about bad girls, fast girls," she said with some bitterness. "I wanted to talk to you about your friend."

I could hardly breathe.

"What happened to you?"

"I was no longer seeing the young man and had no desire to get back together. He was the wrong person; it was the wrong time."

She moved closer to me. "I wish I'd had a close friend to talk to, but I'd only been in the city a short while. There was a woman at work I occasionally had lunch with. She was very nice, I thought." For a brief moment Aunt Sheila was lost in memory. "I hinted to her that I had a girlfriend in trouble. The words were barely out of my mouth when she picked up her purse and left. She said she'd forgotten she had an appointment."

"Did you have to work together?"

"Yes, but we never had lunch again. She was always busy."

This is my Aunt Sheila telling me this. Except for those weeks when Uncle George was drunk after Dad got arrested, I'd never thought much about her.

"What did you do?"

"That's what I want to talk to you about. Your friend, she's your age?"

"She's a little older, seventeen."

Aunt Sheila sat up straight. "If her mother won't tell her, you tell her she's not a slut," she said. "And believe me, that's what they'll say to her. *Loose, fast, a slut.*" She looked angry. "A mistake, an accident, however it happened . . ." Aunt Sheila cleared her throat, "she should know she has a choice." Her hands were clasped in her lap. "You said last night you don't know what she wants. Well, I hope she can talk with her mother." She looked directly at me. "As I hope you would if you ever need help."

"Not me!" I said loudly.

Aunt Sheila looked startled.

"I mean—" what *do* I mean?—"I . . . I won't need help."

Aunt Sheila nodded. "And if your friend needs a name, there's a woman—"

"Mrs. Hanson?"

Aunt Sheila blinked rapidly. "No. Someone in Brooklyn. Someone," she paused, "your mother doesn't know."

Rooms with hidden corners.

Wide angle, dark room. A cone of light on a small circle. Mrs. Brooklyn and Aunt Sheila huddle around a cot. Mrs. Brooklyn wears a nurse's hat. "Fear not!" She sings an undiscovered aria written by a famous Italian composer. A steaming kettle sits on a burner in front of a mirror. Camera moves in close. Steam from the kettle fogs the mirror. Mrs. Brooklyn reads from *The Rubaiyat of Omar Khayyam*. A moving finger writes "SHEILA" on the mirror, and, having writ, moves on.

"First your friend will need a pregnancy test, and I can give you the phone number of a doctor who'll do the test," Aunt Sheila said. "She will have to say she's married, or at least engaged."

"But you, you weren't married."

"No," she said thoughtfully. "I wasn't, but I had a friend in Chicago whose husband was a doctor. He gave me the name of someone here." She spoke as if it was the most natural thing in the world to help a friend.

A curtain of silence enveloped us. Then she added, "Jamie, please, this conversation is between you and me." She looked right at me. "Between us," she repeated slowly.

"Sure." I tried to sound casual, like a friend might. But this is my aunt who's my mom's age, and she just told me something no one else in the family knows.

Three people, three secrets.

Aunt Sheila wrote down a name and number and handed it to me. "Thanks," I said, and I really meant it. I gave her a hug, grabbed my books, and left.

16.

Aunt Sheila. I can't get over what she told me. Paul tried to get my attention in trig class. Lunch period I'll leave him a note about Dad. My brain feels fractured.

I stood in the caf entrance but didn't see Paul. Fingers crossed he's waiting on line and out of sight, and it's safe to go to the *Record* room.

Outside the office door I could hear the radio. The Platters were singing about being a great pretender. Pretending? Lying I call it. My song.

This is ridiculous. I'll leave a note at his locker. I turned away just as the door opened, and of course it was Paul.

"Hey, Jamie, I was going to look for you in the cafeteria."

I had to bite my tongue to keep from laughing hysterically. Get it over with. Deep breath.

"My dad says he'll talk with you, but it has to be today after school."

I really don't want this to happen. It feels wrong that Dad won't talk with me, but he will with Paul.

"Any chance we can do it tomorrow? I've a meeting after school."

I stared at him. "My dad said today. Your choice. Gotta go."

He yelled after me, "Okay, okay. See you at the side entrance at 3:20."

I nodded and waved with the back of my hand as I walked down the hall.

Dad was reading in the living room. He looked over the top of the newspaper and motioned us to the couch.

I headed for my room.

"Jamie," Dad said, "please stay."

"Didn't think you wanted me to know about this."

How humiliating. I sound like a whining seven-year-old.

"It's a test to see if you can help interview someone you're close to," Paul said. He has an irritating talent of raising one eyebrow while the other lowers. "So, can you?"

"I hate tests," I said in a low voice, but I put my books down. "I'm staying only to listen."

"Your choice," Paul said in a mild tone.

I gave him what I hoped was a serious dirty look.

He was all business. Out came the notebook and pencil. He flipped pages and looked up at Dad. "Mr. Morse, I really appreciate this chance to talk with you. I saw the McCarthy committee hearing on television when you pleaded the First—"

"I know taking a plea is a legal phrase," Dad said, "but I vastly prefer saying that I *asserted* my First Amendment rights."

Paul nodded. "Point taken, sir."

I settled back into the softness of the couch. Times like this I like Dad's pedantry. *Correct away, Pops!*

"Do you consider yourself a 'political prisoner'?" Paul asked, poised to write down Dad's answer.

"Well." Dad folded up his paper and set it on the little table next to his chair. "I'm accused and convicted of a crime. But what kind of crime did I commit? I didn't rob a bank. I didn't break into someone's home. I didn't physically attack anyone. I certainly didn't commit murder. What have I done? I don't have guns hidden under my sofa, but I do have ideas in my head. And I've taken political positions some people don't like."

"Unfortunately for you, important people," Paul said.

"Sadly." Dad nodded. "So I'm named as a Communist, and the Communist Party is a *political* party. I'm then fired from my job because of that *political* name-calling. And in this country right now one isn't simply identified as a Communist, one is vilified." Dad looked carefully at Paul to see if he understood.

"Maligned," Paul said.

Of course. "Vilify" had been one of Paul's words in the *Record* office when he rejected an attack piece on the head of the cafeteria. "Just tell the story," he said. "No need to *vilify*. The facts are damning enough."

Dad looked like he was enjoying this exchange. "Then I'm summoned to testify before Senator McCarthy's subcommittee, part of the *political* structure of our government. The Senator orders me to name names of people I supposedly know are Communists. Footnote here," and Dad makes what looks like an asterisk in the air, "naming names is a form of name-calling these days."

Paul wrote furiously in his notebook. So far nothing about life in prison, which is what I'm afraid to hear about.

"I told the Senator I believe that in a democracy no one should be forced *under compulsion of law* to say how he voted, what church, if any, he attends, et cetera, et cetera. You don't like my beliefs, fine. But I've a right to them and, equally important, the right to express them without fear of government harassment.

"Bottom line," Dad continued, "it's none of your business. And if I won't tell you about my political convictions, surely you understand I won't talk about anyone else's." Dad stretched his feet out in front of him and lightly tapped the arms of the chair. "I believe in democracy and free speech, and I condemn any government that gags the speech of its citizens."

Paul's pencil was suspended in midair. "But haven't you supported the Soviet system, which is a dictatorship?"

Dad took a deep breath. "When the revolution happened, I was so hopeful. Many of us were. We thought the world had finally found a way to end poverty." Dad blinked rapidly, his eyes like windshield wipers clearing a mist. "Some people say we were naïve. Perhaps, but I still believe it was a worthy ideal."

"But now we know," Paul said, "Stalin ran a murderous regime." Dad shook his head as if in disgust. "A complete betrayal of the ideals of the revolution."

This is so weird, because Dad left the Communist Party back in 1939 at the time of the Stalin-Hitler pact, way before Senator McCarthy questioned him. Paul didn't know that, and actually I hadn't either until he was fired.

"But Dad," I said, "you weren't even in the party when Senator McCarthy went after you."

"It's okay for you, Jamie, and you, Paul, to ask me about my politics, but not for the government. If members of the John Birch Society—a conservative, vehemently anti-Communist group—were called before Congress, I believe they too have the right not to testify.

"So, I refused to answer Senator McCarthy's questions, and boom! I'm charged with 'Contempt of Congress.' It took over two years until final sentencing." Dad folded his arms across his chest. "So, yes, I'd say it's accurate to call me a political prisoner."

Dad's eyes half-closed the way they do when he goes off somewhere. I looked down at Scruffy, who had his head and one paw on my lap, the other paw tucked under his belly. His eyes were also half-closed, and he blinked. Someone once told me that's how cats send you a kiss.

I felt better.

"In prison, Mr. Morse," Paul said, "was there a difference between how you and other prisoners were treated, since you were in there because of your ideas?"

Here it is! All energy vacuumed out of my arms and legs. I no longer felt better.

```
A barbed-wired yard....
    Tough-looking   men   in   bunches,   leaning
against the wall....
    Tight close-up on striped shirt with bull's-
eye on back....
    Striped pants torn....
    Two guards, grinning, walk slowly towards
inmate....
```

"Behind bars is not a place you want to be," Dad said, "but the actual conditions in this minimum-security prison weren't that bad." His mouth curled in a half smile. "Mind you, I'm not talking about the food. Dreadful."

"So it wasn't like in a James Cagney movie," Paul said, "with guards whacking their batons on the cell gates, itching to beat up inmates?"

Dad shook his head. "No, but I'm sure there are many prisons much worse than anything Cagney ever acted in. Just not this one."

Paul picked at the eraser on his pencil. At one of our first editorial meetings at the *Record*, he had told us about his interviewing technique: if there's an awkward silence, let it happen. Don't rush in to fill up the space. Let *them*. You might get something really quotable.

But this isn't a space; it's a chasm. And it's my dad.

Dad broke the silence. "We were a mixed bunch, and we all knew why each of us was there. Sure, there were some guards and inmates who'd yell 'Better dead than red!' And there was a little bit of shoving, but mostly we'd all spend our time getting through our time. And part of the daily routine was crossing off days on a makeshift calendar."

Dad rubbed his hands up and down the arms of the chair. "I missed this."

"Your chair?" I said.

He smiled again.

"Were there a lot of political prisoners?" Paul asked.

"Three of us. Most of the others had committed what they call 'white-collar' crimes. They'd stolen from a business, bribed someone, lied to stock investors, perjured themselves about something, those kinds of non–physically violent crimes."

Paul stopped writing. "So the other inmates weren't really scary-looking people."

Dad tapped his fingertips together. "This wasn't like a maximum-security prison where people are doing hard time. A lot of those inmates are not only tough, but they want to look that way. Offense, some say, is the best defense for survival. Very different from the group I was with."

Dad looked out the window. When he turned back to us, his voice wavered, his words no longer sharp and distinct. "The truth is there *is* something awful about prison."

Run!

"But it wasn't physical brutality."

Scruffy leapt off the couch. Did he know what was coming? I watched him as he trotted down the hallway.

"It's all about doors," Dad said. "Opened and locked by someone you don't know. And you don't have the key."

Dad looked at me and Paul, but I don't think he was seeing us. "Until I was behind bars, I never fully appreciated what it means to be free." He leaned forward. "We make choices all the time. We walk down the street when we want. We eat when we're hungry. We stay up late, reading well into the night. But we don't think about these as choices. We live them."

The three of us sat without talking until we were wrapped in the darkening afternoon and Dad had to turn on the table lamp.

17.

11:35. I'm getting to be a stickler about time. Six blocks from the subway to Lois's stoop. Lois said two of her friends would be there, Mary something and Phyllis something.

Lois was alone in the kitchen when I came in. "Hey, Jamie, slight change in plans. It's just you and me."

"Hey," I said. How is it your voice can crack on one word?

Run!

She looked at me quizzically, and I looked at my watch and gave a half smile. "Got a train in an hour and a half."

She seemed to accept that and steered me to her couch. "Put your feet up, kiddo. It's not much time, and I've got some phone numbers for you." She went back into the kitchen and returned with a plate of cookies, a teapot, and a pad tucked under her arm.

"Might as well get started," she said, and the knot in my chest loosened a little. "But there's one ground rule, Jamie. This is information only for you and friends who need it. Mind you, it's not shame or guilt, or anything like that. It's the world out there." She grabbed a cookie. "Think of this room as a separate universe," she said.

"Rooms with hidden corners," I murmured to myself.

"Any chance Elaine would go to California?" she asked. "I've got some numbers there she could call."

I shook my head. "Her father's got her chained at home. Won't even let her come into Manhattan."

"Chained?" Lois said, startled.

"He watches her every move. She has to go into the bathroom to be alone, and it's tough because the phone cord doesn't go that far."

Lois flipped some pages on the pad. "Well, here's one thing she could try at home. Vodka and 7-UP."

I pictured Elaine staggering around, tipsy from the vodka and hiccupping from the 7-UP bubbles.

My damn eye began twitching again, and Lois's voice seemed to come through an echo chamber.

"It sounds slightly nauseating, I know, but apparently it does work for some people," she said.

"What does?"

"Vodka and 7-UP." She looked at me sharply. "Are you okay?"

"Right. I'll tell her."

I have no idea if Elaine's parents have vodka. Probably. Even mine do, and they don't drink a lot.

Lois turned more pages. "Here's a number for a doctor in New Jersey, but if Elaine can't travel—"

"We'll figure out a way," I said.

She wrote the number on a blank page, tore it out of the pad, and handed it to me.

"Officially, he doesn't do abortions, and she doesn't want one."

I must have looked confused.

"With different doctors you say different things, but they're all something like 'I'm bleeding a lot,' or 'I've funny pains every month.' Doesn't much matter. They know."

This is getting complicated, and I feel very dumb. I'm glad Elaine isn't here. For sure she'd be out the door by now.

"And prepare her that the doctor may tell her not to get undressed, except for her pants, of course." Lois shook her head slightly. "Happened to a friend of mine. 'In case you have to leave quickly,' the doctor told her."

"Oh no!" I covered my mouth.

```
Wide angle, dark room. A cone of light on a
small circle. This time a girl, not Aunt Sheila,
lies on a kitchen table, fully dressed, her legs
spread apart. She is singing in her head every
showtune she knows, trying to calm down, to
keep her pounding heart from bursting out of
```

```
her chest. But she's afraid she won't hear the
police, so she stops singing. The stillness is
shattered by a siren howling—
```

"Stop!" I said softly and shook my head to get rid of
the picture. I so didn't want to see that movie.

"You sure you're okay?" Lois leaned toward me.

I nodded. And blushed.

"More tea?" she asked.

I nodded again, afraid I'd croak if I tried to speak.
Lois went to fill the pot, and I got up and walked around
the living room. I needed to move. If being grown-up is
hearing stories like this, I'd like to wait a little.

"Sometimes you grow up fast," she said as she brought
back a refilled teapot and a plate of cookies. "Elaine," she
paused, "and you, too."

My face felt hot. I didn't want her to sit next to me
on the couch, so I sat in an armchair, the kind that's deep
enough you can sink in and almost disappear.

"If you can find a private doc, it's best," Lois said, "because with some hospitals you have to convince their staff
psychiatrists you'd kill yourself if they don't help you."

"You're kidding!"

Is that what Mom and Aunt Sheila were talking about?
If the hospital wouldn't help, maybe Mrs. Hanson could?

"And some hospitals sterilize you at the same time
they give you the abortion."

"*Sterilize?*"

She took a deep breath. "Bastards. Making sure you'll never be able to have another baby."

I grabbed a cookie. Something sweet. Something soothing. Something decent.

"Remember *The Philadelphia Story*, with Katharine Hepburn, Jimmy Stewart, and Cary Grant?" I said.

"Yup."

"There's the scene when you find out nothing happened between Stewart and Hepburn, and she asks him, 'Why? Was I so unattractive?' And he says, 'Not at all. But you were a little the worse for drinking, and there are rules about things like that.'" I leaned back, exhausted. "Elaine sleeps with Neil and she gets pregnant—" I started to cry "—and now she has to be crazy to get help. Isn't anyone like Jimmy Stewart?"

"Hey, Jamie, it'll be okay. She'll work it out. Listen, you never know how parents will be when you really need them. Sometimes they come through. There are good people out there."

Mrs. Reilly, the Kotex-counter? Mr. Reilly on Elaine-stakeout?

Mom? Dad?

Lois looked up from her pad. "Like Robert Spencer, the local doc in Ashland, a small town in Pennsylvania—broken bones, sore throats, births—everything. He takes care of people with all kinds of problems." She repeated, *"All kinds of problems.* There are brave ones like him who risk going to jail. Here's his number." She tore a page from the pad.

"Women go to him from all over the country. He charges maybe fifty dollars, or whatever you can pay. A truly decent man." She handed me the paper. "Only problem is you can't always be sure he's there. I had a friend who went, but the office was closed. There was a note tacked to the front door: 'On vacation.' He was supposed to be in, but the police often warn him of a scheduled raid." She paused. "And why not? Cops' wives and girlfriends also get pregnant."

I scrambled to think of how to get Elaine out of New York. I pictured the two of us riding a bus deep into the Pennsylvania countryside.

"He's an amazing man," Lois said. "He has rooms in his office for Negro girls who can't find a place to stay in Ashland."

My head was spinning with everything I didn't know. I must have looked weird, for Lois got up from the couch and started to come over to me. I stood up quickly. "Gotta go. Thanks." And I was out the door.

Lois should have watched out for me. . . . She should have watched out for me. . . . She should have watched out for me. The words a refrain over the grinding of the subway wheels.

Then suddenly a flood I could not stop.

I could not run.

18.

TIME: Almost two months ago.

SETTING: Lois took me to one of her favorite places in the Village, the Peacock Café, where according to tradition the cobwebs date from the roaring twenties and the cheesecake is divine.

SCENE: We drank coffee and ate the famous cheesecake, me and Lois and Stella, Lois's friend, and then this guy walks in and joins us, just like that. He had a wool scarf around his neck. Unshaven and hair kind of shaggy over his ears. Thin, gorgeous, and he made me nervous. Lois asked him whether he'd been to the Ginsberg poetry reading at some bar.

"Uh huh." He looked over her shoulder, and I couldn't tell if he actually was seeing something or pretending faraway thought. He turned his hooded eyes back to Lois. "You should've been there."

"So, Jonas, this is my cousin Jamie." She nodded toward me. "She's an artist," she smiled at him, then me, "and quite talented. Why don't you come over? We're going to have a early dinner before she goes home."

"Why not?" he said. He took out two cigarettes, tapped the ends on the table, put them both in his mouth, lit them, and handed one to Stella, who batted her eyelashes.

Now, Voyager with Paul Henreid lighting Bette Davis's cigarette. I thought I'd faint.

Jonas closed and opened his eyes unbearably slowly. He tilted his head as if peering deep into me. I poked at my cheesecake. Faker, said my head, but the rest of me tingled. He left, and I felt relieved.

"He's a good friend, but a pretty lousy actor," Stella said.

"We'd never tell him that," Lois added, "and we do go to any performance he's in."

"Mercifully, not many," Stella said, rolling her eyes.

Lois laughed. "You're terrible."

They split the bill, and I walked with Lois back to her apartment.

"Have you known him a long time?"

"Jonas? Three years, maybe four. He can come on a little strong with those half-closed eyes," she laughed, "but he's a decent guy."

"But did you ever . . ." my voice was almost a whisper "sleep with him?"

"Oh no, sweetie, we're just friends. I laughed the first time he whispered sweet nothings in my ear, and we've been friends ever since. If I were in any kind of trouble, I'm sure he'd be there for me."

"Hey just friends, sure, hey . . ." I dribbled on and suddenly realized Lois wasn't next to me. I looked back and she was smiling.

"We're having dinner, that's all," she said. "Think of Jonas as an actor auditioning to get you to like him. That, after all, is what most actors are doing, no? So relax, it's okay."

I didn't feel at all relaxed and definitely not okay. We walked on in silence.

Not long after we were back in the apartment, there he was, holding a bag of donuts.

The afternoon is a blur. He and Lois chatted about people and things I didn't know. Every once in a while he'd look at me and smile. A sleepy, soft smile. I started sketching them both. When I'm on the subway drawing people, I try to read personalities from the way they cross or don't cross their legs. Men and women are very different. Lois was on the couch, lying on her side, legs folded, her cheek pressed against her hand. Jonas was in the armchair, legs straight out, planted about two feet apart. His arms hung down over the sides of the chair. The only thing I read from this: they were both ready for a nap.

I was so absorbed in my crosshatching I didn't realize Jonas had gotten up and was standing next to me until he cast a shadow over my sketch.

"There's a gallery opening tonight. Pencil work. Interested?"

"Me? . . . I mean we . . . I . . . I mean—"

"Jamie, sweetie," Lois said, "you can stay over here tonight. Call home and tell them. I'm going to a poetry reading, but I think you'll enjoy the pencil-art exhibit more. And Jonas," she said in a mock serious tone, "be nice to my cousin."

With his eyes half-closed, Jonas stood waiting for my answer.

I nodded.

"I'll skip dinner," he said. "See you later."

So I called home about staying over and Mom said fine and Lois went down to pick up a few things for dinner and I stayed in her apartment and read I don't remember what and then I scraped

carrots and peeled potatoes and Lois made some
kind of stew with everything and then we ate.

Do I sound nervous?

Jonas was coming "circa seven-thirty" he
had said.

Lois kept saying, "I'm so glad you're going
to the opening. I've seen that artist's work.
You'll connect with it."

She chatted about the artist, and I followed
her into the bathroom where she put on make-up.

"You want to borrow my eyeliner when
I'm done?"

I'd never used eyeliner. I never saw my
mother use eyeliner. My aunt doesn't use eyeliner. What kind of house did I grow up in?

"Sure," I said, as if putting on eyeliner
were an everyday event.

I figured she'd put it on and I'd watch. It
was the beginning of an evening of deception.

"Eyeliner was first used in Ancient Egypt
and in the Fertile Crescent area. I wrote a poem
about it," she said.

It's amazing what I'm learning this weekend.

When it was my turn, I nearly stabbed myself
in my right eye, but by then Lois was gone and
I was on my own.

"Let me know what you think of the exhibit,"
she'd said as she left for her reading. I walked

around the apartment trying to calm down. I'd stare at myself every time I passed the hallway mirror. Who was that girl with black-circled eyes, hair behind one ear, in front of the other? Lois had thought that looked interesting.

Everything made me nervous—looking interesting, Jonas looking the way he did, Lois smiling and calling me an artist.

At last he arrived and we left. As we walked down Bleecker Street, he took my hand and put it in his jacket pocket with his. "Put me in your pocket, Mike," Katharine Hepburn had said to Jimmy Stewart.

The gallery was overflowing. Lots of men who looked like Jonas and nobody, I was sure, who looked like me. A long table at the end had several big jugs of red wine and stacks of paper cups. Baskets of crackers sat at the ends of the table. In between were large rounds that were definitely not Swiss or American cheeses. I heard a woman say the dripping brie was delicious, and that's how I learned the cheese was called dripping brie.

Definitely learning a lot.

Jonas handed me a cup of wine. It wasn't his fault, really. On the way over I'd lied and told him about my eighteenth birthday and how the weather had been bleak but the time glorious.

So I'd added almost two years, so what? Well, the "so what" is here I was with a cup of red wine in one hand, as common an occurrence for me as putting on eyeliner. The wine scratched my throat as it went down. Was it supposed to? What did dripping brie taste like?

I never found out. Jonas had his hand on my shoulder and steered me through the crowd. Every once in a while he'd stop and say hello to someone. The men usually ignored me, the women looked. Jonas said I'd just arrived in town. "Are you staying long?" one woman with a long black braid woven with colored ribbons asked. But she turned away before I had a chance to say anything. A couple of women gave me a quick sweep always followed by a slight smile. I'm sure I didn't pass whatever test it was. I didn't think anyone ever looked you over from head to toe, but I guess that's why there's the expression. I felt woozy, and my stomach gurgled from the wine.

"Let's split," Jonas said softly in my ear. His warm breath, the cushion of his voice—I...I think his tongue brushed my ear. He tucked my arm under his, and I tried to keep my head up high as he led us through the crowd.

The silence on the street, a relief, was broken by a car horn blast. I didn't ask where we were going; I was just relieved my legs were working. We turned on a narrow street and went down several steps. Jonas pushed open a door. The room was dimly lit, mainly from flickering candles. We were directed to a small table in a corner. A Chianti bottle in the center of the checkered tablecloth was covered with wax drippings. Jonas ordered two hamburgers and a half bottle of wine.

"I ate already," I murmured.

He didn't seem to care.

As for the wine, well.

Here's the thing. I don't know what time we left. I was sleepy and couldn't stop myself from grinning on and off like a blinking neon sign. I began to giggle uncontrollably. We climbed a thousand flights of stairs to his apartment, one room, foldout couch folded out. His clothes were dropped in a random pattern around the room. I desperately needed the bathroom.

"It's mine only, so here's the key." Jonas sent me out into the hallway and pointed to a door with a poster painting of triangles that I think dripped green blood.

When I came back, Jonas was stretched out on the couch-bed. He shoved aside some magazines and patted an empty space. I sat down. He is great-looking. Very gently he pulled me down next to him. He moved a few inches away and put his hands behind his head.

A little necking. Second base, that's it. I can handle this, I said to myself.

"So," he said.

"So," I said back, feeling very clever.

He turned me on my side and held my face in both his hands. His lips were cloud-soft as he pressed me close to him. His hands swept my shoulders and down my back.

Then he was on top of me. He lifted my sweater and unhooked my bra.

"Please," I said. "Don't!"

I pushed. I said no. He kissed me. Hard. I twisted. I wrenched an arm free and punched. He laughed and held me down. I begged. I yelled. And I watched it all from above.

Him and the Girl.

Her sweater comes off and She is on her back with Him on top. He presses her arms down. I rise up higher for a wide-angle view. The shades aren't pulled down, but it is dark. The window faces a brick wall. It might be early morning. You can't tell.

Pan back to the couch. The Girl has her knees up and legs bent. The Girl tries to twist free. She spits at him. He frees a hand for a quick moment and slaps Her. Then he holds Her in that position. He grunts. She looks straight up. Dull eyes. Open.

Then it was over. He rolled on his back.

I couldn't move. I hurt like I'd been cut with a knife. Searing. I wanted to scream. I couldn't make a sound.

"So it really was your first time. Some girls like it rough." There was a smile in his voice. "But you'll learn to like it."

I wanted to throw up. Why hadn't he stopped when I said no? My head pounded. I slipped on my sweater and looked for my pants on the floor. He smoked and talked, asked me questions. I wouldn't speak. I wouldn't answer. I had to leave. He kept talking.

"Why the rush?" He offered me his cigarette. "First times are special." He blew a smoke ring.

I left.

Outside I asked someone how to get to Lois's street. It was still dark. "Can you tell me the time?" I said to the young woman who'd given me directions.

"One fifteen." She hurried off.

Lois looked like I'd woken her up. "Hey kid, have fun?" She peered at me in the dark foyer, then turned and sat down at the kitchen table.

She rubbed her eyes. "What time is it?"

All I could say was, "Tired, very tired."

She'd ask a question and I'd nod or shake my head. No words. If I opened my mouth, I knew I'd scream and never stop. Around two she went to bed and I curled up in a ball on the couch. I lay there until light streaked through the blinds. Then I dressed quickly.

Lois brought me a cup of coffee, but I couldn't take anything in. "I'll come with you to the station," she said.

I shook my head. She reached for me but I pulled away. How could she not have known?

I left and she didn't try to follow me.

On the subway ride home, I nodded like people swaying in church. My prayer—please god, let nobody be home!

The door was locked top and bottom, a good sign.

For the time being, safe.

I took a shower, a very long one, and let the hot water beat on my face. Someday I'll talk again. Then I went to bed.

MAY

19.

It felt as if it had happened yesterday instead of months ago. Memory floods will do that to you, I guess. I avoided Lois's calls. She left a couple of messages with Mom, which I ignored. And I'd gotten the shortest letter I think Elaine has ever written: "My parents know."

I think I'd be happy if I never got another letter or phone call as long as I live.

At school I'd been working on yearbook sketches, so most days I brought lunch and ate in the art room. Georgina and Kay had been rehearsing for the drama club play, and Carol had an after-school chemistry project. Not a lot of time to talk, which was fine by me. Busy was wonderful.

At home everybody worried about Dad, but nobody said anything. He'd go on job interviews a couple of times a week, and a couple of times a week he'd be rejected. He barely talked at dinner, and he hasn't listened much. Mom has tried to get him going. She'll be sarcastic, or make a joke, or play devil's advocate about something he used to care about, but he doesn't seem to want to be reached. It's getting to her. I'm not sure Stevie's noticed, but Uncle Maury has. He thinks Mom should leave Dad alone. "Rachel, you've got to give him space," he said when he was drying dishes one night. "It's a helluvan adjustment. He'll come around."

Mom wasn't buying it. "You don't get it, Maury. You can't get a job if you walk in like a defeated sad sack. A dog-catcher applicant has to convey more interest."

Sad-sack not-even-dogcatcher, my very smart dad. We haven't talked alone since Paul was here. I thought that had changed something, but he's pulled back from me along with everyone else. But there is one thing that's changed. I've stopped seeing bull's-eye targets on a prison back. And barbed wire has turned into doors.

Yet even with all the attention on Dad, I bet I'm the only one who's noticed that he goes around opening them when they're closed. Sometimes Stevie or Grandma or even Mom makes him re-shut the door. Not me. I let it stay open.

The one plus is Dad's state of mind is center stage, so nobody has paid much attention to me. Except for Grandma. She'll make a big deal of putting an extra-large slice of cake in front of me. Sometimes she'll look at me and her eyebrows will go up and down as if trying to send signals into my brain. I've never been able to lie to Grandma, so I've been coming home too late for tea and cookies.

But you can hold things in only so long. One day when I got home earlier than usual, Uncle Maury was there. We'd had one of those sex-education classes in school, which was hard to watch. But I could talk to Uncle Maury about a lot of different things. Besides, like I said, you can hold things in only so long.

"So you don't think it's wrong?"

"Premarital sex? No. Why?" Uncle Maury answered in a measured voice. "Your friend?"

"In hygiene class," I said, "they showed us a movie about giving birth. The girl next to me looked like she was going to faint."

Uncle Maury nodded. "It's messy," he said, "and I can understand where it could be hard to look at."

"Afterwards, they gave us a questionnaire, mostly about all the stuff in the film and on eating right so the baby would be healthy and what to feed it after. That kind of thing. But then there was this question about premarital sex and did we think it was okay."

"What did you write?"

"I said, 'Yes, if it's someone you love.'"

"Good answer," Uncle Maury said.

But you'll learn to like it . . .

I thought I'd be sick. I ran for the bathroom and splashed cold water on my face.

"You okay?" Uncle Maury called from the living room.

"Fine. Be right there." I heard the front door open. Must be Mom, or maybe Stevie. Mom had left a note saying Uncle Maury was coming for dinner and one of us should pick up a coffee cake at Baumgarten's Bakery. I hoped Stevie had.

I rinsed my mouth and went back into the living room. Mom was talking to Uncle Maury. She hadn't taken her coat off, but it was already a serious conversation.

"Are you worried about your friend?" she asked me.

Uncle Maury looked up. "I told your mother a little of what we were talking about."

"Yeah, I am. I called her a couple of times this week, and the last time she started to cry. She said they took her to Catholic Services and made her sign some papers." I sat down on the couch. "They're saying she has to give up the baby."

Mom bit her lip. "What a terrible choice."

"The only terrible thing," Uncle Maury said, "is when someone brings an unwanted child into the world."

"But she wants it," I said.

Mom looked confused.

"Her parents, they don't care. The only thing they care about is that she has to have it," I said.

Uncle Maury shook his head. "Whoa, wait a minute. You just said she wants it. And her parents say she has to have it—what's the problem?"

I felt my face getting hot. "You don't understand!" I said, half-yelling. "She wants to *keep* it, not give it away."

"But she's only sixteen," Mom said.

"Seventeen." I started to cry.

Mom sat down next to me on the couch. "Sweetheart." That was all, but it uncorked me. *ME* I wanted to shout, but I could talk only about Elaine.

"None of you get it! She really loves her boyfriend—and now he won't talk to her—and she wants to marry him—and he won't answer her calls—and she wants his baby—and her parents say no—and she was going to go to college—and we were going to go together—and she doesn't even care about that anymore—and what's going to happen to her—and the guy won't even talk to her, the bastard—and she doesn't want to talk to me and . . ." I hiccupped violently and it slipped out . . . "What's going to happen to me?"

Dad stood in the doorway. Stevie was behind him with the bakery box. I stared at Dad and yelled. "And you, you don't think about anybody but yourself. You're here but you disappear. Why did you even come home?" I slumped back against Mom. "And now my friend's going to disappear."

Dad sat down in the big chair. Stevie stood frozen, holding the coffee cake.

Mom held me. She was crying. Grandma watched all of us from the foyer.

"Why aren't *you* crying," I yelled at Dad.

Mom wiped her eyes. I didn't move. Dad sighed.

"What a mess!" Grandma said. And she was right. "A regular Niagara Falls!" She went into the kitchen and brought out a pot of soup.

"Soup and coffee cake. What could be bad?" Uncle Maury said.

I wasn't hungry and went to my room. I had a pile of homework I didn't want to look at. *What's going to happen to me?* A good thing nobody picked up on that, because I'm not ready for the really big lie. I will never tell anyone, ever, about . . . I can't even say his name.

A hundred years ago in the cafeteria Carol said no way she could give birth and give it up. Elaine says she wants to keep it. She says I don't understand. Maybe she's right. I felt dizzy. What's right for her? For me? For anybody? How do you know?

"May I come in?"

I looked up. Dad stood in the doorway.

"I guess."

I stayed at my desk. Dad sat on the bed.

"What—"

"I—"

We started and ended at the same moment. Dad looked serious.

"Jamie," he said. "What did you mean by 'What's going to happen to me?'"

He'd heard.

"Nothing. I didn't mean anything. Really."

"Whenever anyone says 'Really' with a capital R, I wonder."

I can't make Dad out. Maybe he *is* here more than he seems. "I was thinking about me after graduation," a weak lie, "and I really am sorry for what I said about your coming home." That was the truth.

He made an it-doesn't-matter gesture with his hands.

"I mean it. I really am glad you're home." And the next thing I knew I was sitting next to him, crying on his shoulder.

"Hey, kiddo, what's this? You're so glad I'm home you burst into tears?"

I reached over to the Kleenex box on the little stool next to my bed. I blew hard. "Yeah, that's it." I grabbed another. "Mr. Kleenex must be a pretty rich guy by now."

Dad put his hands around my face. "You can't make your friend's decisions for her, you know. Nothing she does will be easy. It may not be the choice you or I would make. We can't help that."

But what happens when someone takes the choice away from you? I didn't want what happened to me. I had said no. Elaine wanted to be with Neil. And he seems to be saying no.

"The thing is," I said, "she hasn't told her parents she wants to keep the baby. They're deciding everything, and they're not interested in anything she wants. It's me she's told, and she screamed at me when I said, 'Why don't you tell them?' She said she couldn't. They told her she's ruined *their* life. I said, 'What about yours?' and she hung up on me."

Dad sat for another moment, then stood up. "Come, let's have soup. Comfort food."

I could use some of that.

20.

I heaved the chemistry book into my locker. Georgina and Carol were at the other end of the hall. Some secrets you don't share. "Not mine, not Elaine's."

The kid at a nearby locker looked at me. "You say something?"

I shook my head. I must look like a nut, talking to myself.

Now that the yearbook work was over, I'd been bringing lunch and eating in the newspaper office. No cafeteria. A special assignment for the *Record*, I'd told them. "Pretty lame," I said sharply. This time the kid at the next locker really freaked out. "Sorry," I said.

It was seventh period, and I headed for the *Record* office to check the schedule. Paul was packing up files when I came in. He looked up and smiled. Would he smile if he knew? Do I look different?

Kay says Herbie says the boys know who the easy girls are, but he won't say who.

I'm not "easy." Elaine's not. Would Paul think we were if he knew? I feel like Hester Prynne in that book we read in English, *The Scarlet Letter.* Hester loved the man she made love with, but the town said she committed adultery. Me? Absolutely no love. They forced Hester Prynne to wear an embroidered scarlet letter *A*. And me?

```
Jamie M. Prynne walks a narrow path between a
crowd of thousands. She does not wear a Scar-
let Letter. Hers is a banner, "SHE WENT ALL THE
WAY!"
    Jamie MP shouts, "I didn't want to" but no
sounds come out of her mouth. The crowd on the
left murmurs, "SHE ASKED FOR IT," those on the
right growl, "SHE WAS AN OCCASION OF SIN!"
```

Suddenly I didn't want to know what Paul thought. I mumbled something and started to leave.

"Hey, Jamie, wait up!"

Please, please don't ask me anything.

But all he wanted to know was when I planned to turn in my story. I would have probably gone on mulling my own awkwardness, but Paul broke the silence. "And I wanted to ask you . . ." he paused and swallowed. "I wanted to ask you if . . . if you want to go to the movies Saturday night?"

He tossed a pencil from hand to hand. Paul, nervous! He's thinking A Real Date, not like the other times we've gone to the movies. I made myself look at him, which was easy because he wasn't looking at me. He's not Him, I told myself. He's Paul, and a friend. And there won't be any wine or dripping brie and neither of us is eighteen. He knows me.

I looked over at the board. "PRELAPSARIAN" was Paul's word of the day. I actually knew it. An innocent, unspoiled time.

I stared at my hands and concentrated as if they held a precious jewel I couldn't let out of my sight: Who I Was Before.

"What's playing?" I said so softly I wasn't sure he'd heard.

"I'll make a list."

Without looking, I knew he was bathed in relief.

At the door I turned back. "Do you know anything about those homes where they send pregnant girls?" It popped out before I had a chance to think.

He blinked in surprise. "Actually, yeah. There's a kid in my building who's adopted, and a couple of weeks ago I got the whole story. Or at least as much as he knows. I didn't get home until late," he pointed to the *Record* files, "and he was hanging out on the stoop, pounding his fist into a baseball mitt. You know me and baseball. He's a Giants fan, so I asked if he was mad that Pee Wee Reese scored off that wide throw by Don Mueller.

"It was as if he hadn't heard me. He said he'd just found out that his mother was alive and that she'd given him up.

He'd always thought she'd died when he was born, and he didn't know which made him feel worse."

"His real mother had been in one of those homes?"

"That's what they told him."

This is going to be Elaine's story, I thought. "Maybe they made her give him up."

"Don't know. But when he told his parents he wanted to find his real mother, they said he couldn't because the files were sealed. Even they don't know who she is, because in those homes they make you change your name. And the adoption papers, which he saw for the first time, have the made-up name."

There's a reason they say your mouth "fell open." Mine did. "What is it with these people? It's not enough they take your baby, but also your name!"

He looked at me quizzically. "Why do you want to know?"

I put it on Lois. "My cousin was telling me about someone she knew."

That seemed to satisfy him. I wanted to go home and climb into bed, my head under the covers.

My last class was study hall. No thinking, nobody calling on you, just waiting for the day to be over. I went into the girls' room, second stall from the left. Scratched on the side wall: DARLENE DOES IT.

Did Darlene love someone? Did she think she was getting married? Maybe she had a bad date and bad wine. They don't tell you those things on a bathroom wall.

21.

I told Paul I'd meet him on my stoop. I said I had an errand to run and wouldn't be in the apartment. It was easier. I couldn't bear the thought of anyone in the family talking to him. Actually Mom wasn't too bad about that kind of thing, and Grandma would sit and smile. She likes Paul. Dad, well. They'd probably start talking about the Senate vote that condemned Senator McCarthy and then prisons and then who knows what else.

But Stevie, he is the dangerous one. He's in the kissing-girls-is-weird stage, and he'd be home.

I waited outside. Stevie burst through the front door of the building and jumped the stoop steps down to the sidewalk. He turned back and grinned. "Hot night, hot lips?"

"I'm going to strangle you!"

And of course Paul arrived at exactly that moment.

Stevie ran down the street, but not before yelling, "Hey Paul, hot night, hot lips!"

"Good idea!" Paul yelled back.

"Stupid, stupid, stupid!" I headed for the corner.

"Hey, he's just a kid," Paul said, catching up with me.

"No excuse!"

He pulled a clipping from his pocket. "I say the new Humphrey Bogart movie, *The Harder They Fall*. The boxing world. What do you think?"

I looked away.

"I know you don't like watching people bash each other around, but it's about—"

I didn't hear what it was about. The harder they fall. Me and Elaine.

I always have a crumpled tissue in my pocket. After a wipe and a blow, I tossed it in the garbage can on the next street corner.

Paul watched me closely. "What's happening?" he said.

"Nothing. You know. Fragile emotions. Girl things." I tried to laugh.

"Okay." He sounded relieved. "So, what do you think about Bogart? The review says he and Rod Steiger are great."

"Why not?"

We walked to the Loew's Palace in silence, and that's something else I like about Paul. We don't feel uncomfortable if we don't feel like talking. Inside the theater,

I went for the seats and he stood on line for popcorn. It was as much of a tradition as we had after going to seven movies. The balcony was where kids went to neck and smoke. I picked two seats in the middle of the orchestra.

I watched Paul as he came down the aisle. He was tall and thin, but nothing else like the Other One. Nothing at all.

The theater darkened, and we shared the popcorn. Newsreel. Coming attractions. I love everything on the big screen. Once those lights go down I'm a happy person.

But not tonight. I kept stealing glances at Paul. He's a good guy, a Jimmy Stewart. I think. Could he ever do something like . . . what happened?

It wasn't a fair question. Paul's been my friend. I didn't know the Other One. I still can't say his name, not even to myself. The Creep. And look at Neil. He won't talk to Elaine. Do you ever really know someone?

The Harder They Fall was bleak. Greed, power, and corruption big-time, with the syndicate fixing boxing matches. Bogart, an out-of-work sportswriter, was hired to make a weak fighter sound like the menace of the Western world. The crisis: what if you've done such a slick job both the world and the fighter himself believe he is that tough? You know he's got a powder-puff punch, and because of you he's going up against a killer. What do you do then?

The fight scenes were brutal. Black and white is more real than color.

Like me right now, black and white.

```
Long shot. The Girl walks down city street. Sun
casts strong shadows. Girl is smiling. Man leans
against stoop railing. Cleans his nails with a
penknife. Whistles a tuneless tune. Says some-
thing to the Girl. Camera moves in to close-up
of her face. Open, trusting. Camera pans over
to the Man. He speaks, but traffic horns drown
out the sound. Man beckons Girl up the stairs.
Screen goes black.
```

"The End" flashed on the big screen. What a mess I am. *The Harder They Fall* could be my title. *A Woman with Dark Secrets* next best. "Melodramatic" they'd say. Right. "Unbelievable storyline," they'd say. Wrong. Autobiographical.

We headed for Jimmy's soda fountain, where we sat in a booth and talked about the movie, the *Record*, classes, the Dodgers and the Giants. Nothing personal. Safe.

The counter boy came over for the order.

"White and black soda," I said.

Paul smiled. "Black and white," he ordered for himself. He grinned at me. "You're the only person I've ever heard order it that way."

The counter boy nodded. "Unique," he said, flipping his pad closed.

"I like chocolate ice cream and vanilla soda better than the other way around."

"Of course." Paul nodded solemnly.

"I'm not trying to be different." I started to cry.

"Fragile emotions still?" Paul said.

I cried some more.

He moved over to my side of the booth and put his arm around my shoulders.

"Listen," he said, "it can't be that bad. I'll give you an extension till mid-next week."

I rolled my eyes and reached for the soda.

"Okay, I know," he said. "It's not that. But an extended deadline can't hurt."

I sat up and tried to read him. His eyes were a deep brown. Warm.

"You're my friend, right?"

"What is this, you need a notarized . . ." The look on my face must have stopped him. "Hey, always." He took my hand and waited.

I pinched the top of the straw. Where do I start?

"You know my cousin Lois." I didn't wait for an answer or look at him, and I knew he wouldn't say anything. He'd wait for me, let me go at my own pace. He held my hand a little tighter, that was all.

"She's got lots of friends, she lives in Greenwich Village, and I went to visit to find out . . ."

Help! This started with Elaine. Do I tell him? "You see, it's . . . it's very complicated," I said in a low voice.

I didn't consciously think *Either I trust him or I stop*, but I must have decided. I pulled my hand away and faced the empty side of the booth. I gripped the soda glass in both hands. The cold was numbing.

"Elaine is pregnant."

Paul and Elaine had become friends, but only because of me. When Dad was arrested, almost nobody sat with me in the cafeteria. They did.

After a long silence he asked, "Is she okay?"

I slumped against the booth. If he'd have said "No way!" I would have pushed him off the seat and gotten out of there as fast as I could.

"Yeah, she's fine . . . no, she's not . . . I don't know." My mouth was dry. I had given away Elaine's biggest secret, and to a boy.

"She wasn't attacked, was she?"

I wanted to scream, I WAS ATTACKED!

"No. It was her boyfriend, and now he won't talk to her."

"What's she going to do?"

"They're making her have the baby and give it away," I said. "Her parents. They're making her." My voice cracked.

Paul put his arm around me again. This time I leaned back into his shoulder.

"So that's why you asked about those homes."

I nodded and blew my nose.

I started to cry again. "Niagara Falls," I blubbered. "My grandma says I'm a regular Niagara Falls."

We sat there together on the same side of the booth, like a movie couple.

And then I told him about me. In one long whoosh with tears, hiccups, shaking.

"*I was attacked.*" My voice was almost a whisper, but I knew he'd heard me because he pulled his arm away. When I looked up, his mouth was open and his back rigid. Scarlet Letter judgment?

"My cousin's friend . . ." I almost choked on the word "took me to a gallery opening. And there was wine. Too much wine." I put my hands over my mouth. What must Paul think?

He touched my shoulder.

"I tried to stop him, I tried, but he didn't listen, he wouldn't stop!"

And that's when Paul gave me a hug.

22.

Carol waited for me at the silverware bins. She pointed to a table in the back against the wall. Georgina and Kay were already there.

"Seems like weeks since you ate with us. It's the newspaper column, right?"

I nodded. "Tons of *Record* work."

The thing about Carol is that if something sounds real she believes it. With my new position she accepted without question that I was busy.

"I'm glad you're back," she said.

Matter-of-fact can be comforting. We headed for the back table.

"Long lost!"

"Found at last!"

"Glad to be here!" I grinned. In truth I was mixed, but chatter was a great distractor.

"You missed me and Herbie in breakup number four," Kay said.

I stared at her. "But you seem so cheerful."

Georgina snorted. "They're back. The break lasted all of forty-five seconds. Question: when is a breakup not a breakup?" She pointed at Kay.

I groaned.

"It lasted a day and a half," Carol said. She dug into the chicken pot pie, always happy to share facts.

"What happened?" I asked.

"Come on, Jamie. The usual fight." Georgina never had much patience for the Kay-and-Herbie Wars.

"Some friend you are," Kay said. "If I didn't like you, I really wouldn't like you."

If the talk stays like this, I can handle it.

Kay sat across from me and leaned forward. "It may seem like same-old same-old to her," she gestured toward Georgina, "but each time Herbie ups the pressure a little, it gets harder to say no."

Georgina sighed. "I suppose."

I'd said no, the bastard, I'd said no!

I scrambled. "What else is new?"

"I'm going to take the practice SAT," Carol said. "After the last Regents, Mr. Morabito said he'd do a test run. Why not, I figure."

"Me too," Georgina said. "And you, Jamie?"

"Hey, if you guys think it's a good idea."

Georgina turned to face me. "You were gung ho about

getting into a good school and going away. Still?"

"Hey, give a girl a break. It's curse cramp time." I'll grab at any excuse.

"Midol's the only thing that helps me," she said. "Anyway, you have to sign up for the session." She went back to her apple pie.

"Hot-water bottle for me," Carol said.

Georgina looked at her. "And you're the practical one? What's she supposed to do in school? Sit with a hot-water bottle?" She turned to me. "I've got Midol with me if you want some."

My cramps weren't of lasting interest. They talked on about the SAT session—they'd all signed up and assumed I would—then summer vacation plans and college sororities Georgina had heard about from her brother. I murmured something now and then; most of the time I was silent due to "cramps."

"Do you want to take some Midol for later?" Georgina asked.

"Midol?" For a moment I'd forgotten. "Sure, that'd be great."

I wrapped the pills in a napkin. We left the caf as the first bell rang. Ten minutes to class.

I had a calendar pasted on the inside of my locker door. It was the only way I could keep track of my schedule. Chemistry now. My bag was behind the chem book. I reached to put the pills away. Nice of Georgina. She didn't have many left. I glanced at the calendar. When's my article due?

Due? DUE!

I'd been so focused on making it through each day, I hadn't noticed. I turned back to last month. The page tore but I held the edges together. I always make a small inked-in triangle on the date I get my period. Upper right-hand corner. I'm not exactly regular, but always within three or four days. I never have missed. Where was the last triangle? I flipped the pages. There it was. Forward. Two months plus late? No! Please, no!

I opened the door of the main office. The assistant behind the desk looked up.

"Yes?"

"Is Nurse Barclay in?"

"Name?"

"Jamie Morse."

She pointed to the bench. "Wait." She disappeared into the inner sanctum.

The door opened and she motioned to me. Nurse Barclay was behind her desk at the end of the room. She was typing and didn't look up.

"The problem?"

"Can I have a pass to go home? I've got really bad cramps," I said. "They're making me nauseous, and they're getting worse." I rubbed my stomach.

"Better cramps than not," she said, continuing to type.

23.

No one was home when I unlocked the front door. The calendar in my room—I looked for the last triangle. How did so much time pass since . . . and I didn't notice?

I tapped my heart as I counted the days. This cannot be right. I couldn't be. Please-tap-No-tap-Please-tap-No-tap-Please-NO!

Grandma was at the Bronx Symphony Orchestra's free concert. She'd talked about it all morning. I ran to her room, the farthest from the front door. A hundred miles farther would have been good. A hundred miles underground even better. A hundred miles anywhere. Please-tap-No!

Grandma's phone sat on the night table next to her bed, dust-free. She hated dust. She took it as a personal challenge that it came back every few days. And then I started shaking.

I knew Lois's number by heart. AG 3-1940. My nail scraped the bottom as I turned the dial. Lois had laughed when I told her it was easy to remember. AGGRAVATION, and 3-1940 is my birthday.

Rings into infinity.

"Lois? It's me. Jamie. Yeah, I . . . no . . . yes, I did get the . . . no, I . . . yes . . . she told me you'd called . . . see, but, . . . Him? No, he wouldn't . . . you didn't give him my number? . . . sure I believe . . . no, you see . . ."

She kept saying I should have called, I should have done this, I should have done that. I should have, I should have, I should have . . .

"You knew him. You're my cousin! He . . . he raped me . . . and I . . . I missed my period." Simple, horrible sentences.

I heard her breathing.

"Jamie, what are you saying? You . . . he . . . why didn't you tell me?"

I stared at the phone.

Her voice cracked. "You don't have too much time."

"What do you mean?"

"To get it done. Under three months. Sometimes two and a half. That's it."

Please. No. Please. No.

"Jamie, are you there? Will your mother help? Jamie? Talk to me. Jamie!"

I hung up.

My heart pounded. I started to sweat. I went to my

room and closed the door. There are no locks. I wish there were locks, oh, I wish there were locks.

Think, Jamie. Think. Breathe. In, out, in, out.

A list. Paper. Pencil.

Time she said. Little time.

Hurry!

How do I find out for sure? Aunt Sheila's doctor for the test. Please, no, please! I pushed the chair back. I paced the room. I banged the bureau. My fist hurt. I looked at the paper. My writing was crooked. I sat down. More crooked writing.

Tell Mom and Dad? They wouldn't say I ruined everything. They wouldn't send me away. Disappointed, that's what they'd say. I hate that word.

I don't want a . . . a baby. Not now. When I'm married.

I don't want to get married. Not now.

I want to graduate next year.

I want to go to college.

Most of all I wanted to sleep.

24.

The phone ring jerked me awake. My stomach turned over, the old feeling from when Dad was away. But Dad's here. I touched my stomach. Me? Pregnant? That's crazy! I sat at the edge of the bed, seven rings. I ran into Grandma's room.

"Jamie?"

"Elaine? What is it?"

"I just bought a ticket. My train gets in in fifty-two minutes. Can you meet me?"

I stood up. My skirt was wrinkled with sleep. I'd change.

"See you."

An hour later a definitely pregnant Elaine got off the train. Her sweater buttons and the holes were at war. We hugged almost long distance. I wanted to look at her belly but didn't dare. We headed for the Automat. I had coffee, Elaine had milk.

"You don't drink tea anymore?" That was almost the first thing I said after the hurried hello in the station.

She didn't answer me till we sat down. She maneuvered herself into the chair. I saw her through my sketching eye. She sat slightly tilted back and reached to put her glass down on the table. I so don't want to look like that.

She put her hand on top of her belly and said, "Only good things for my baby."

This can't be happening.

"Elaine, hello. You don't have a baby. You've got a pre-baby in you. Not a baby."

"A baby, Jamie, it's a baby and it's mine."

"Is a tadpole a frog?"

She looked appalled. "How can you talk like that?"

"How can *you*? Wait a minute, you're right, I'm wrong. A tadpole has a life, swimming around in the *outside* world. *That*," I pointed at her, "is not in the world." I didn't stop. "And besides, it's not going to be yours."

She smiled, as if I were a radio program and she had turned off the sound.

"Elaine, what is going on?"

"I know in my heart that Neil will love this baby and he'll marry me. This is Neil Jr."

Am I crazy or is she?

"They're sending you someplace where they will take the baby away from you. Take it away. Forever. You give it up. You sign papers. They even make you change your name, for Pete's sake!"

She stared at me. "What do you mean?"

This was so weird. Elaine was my oldest friend. I didn't know whether to laugh or scream.

"Somebody told me that, I don't remember who." It was a little lie, not that it matters—but how many little lies make a big one that does matter?

Elaine tilted forward. "Did she go to a Catholic Services home?"

I must have looked puzzled.

She repeated the question slowly, emphasizing each word equally, as if talking to a five-year-old. "Did-she-go-to-a-Catholic-Services-home?"

"I don't know."

"Probably a Florence Crittenton one," she said. "They don't do that in the Catholic homes." She tilted back again with a satisfied smile.

"How do you know that?"

She drained the milk glass. Elaine, who was always so neat, sat with a white mustache and never lifted her napkin. "You wait and see. Neil will take me away, and we'll get married."

You don't stare at someone you think is going crazy, but I did. "Your parents are okay with you and Neil getting married?"

She stopped smiling. "I haven't told them yet. It doesn't matter. I wrote to Neil and told him I'd send the address as soon as I'm there. He'll come and get me."

"Did he answer you?"

"He will."

"I think I'm pregnant," I said. It flew out of my mouth. A reach for reality.

Elaine stared at me.

"I was . . . I was raped." I said, "and I'm not getting married and I don't want it and I'm going to find someone to help me."

I can't believe that came out of me.

"Oh God, Jamie. That's awful!" She reached across the table and touched my hand. "You can come with me!" she said, a tremor in her voice. "You don't have to be Catholic. They help everyone."

"I was attacked, Elaine. This is not the way a child should be born."

We sat; neither of us moved or spoke.

"You've got a white mustache," I said.

She blinked twice and carefully wiped it away. Something had ended.

"I came to tell you," she said, "that I'm leaving in a couple of weeks, and this was my only chance to see you and say goodbye." Her voice became formal. "The next time we meet I'll be Mrs. Neil Jentiss."

25.

It was a long subway ride home, and here's what I saw. A play, not a movie.

Elaine's in a room with a group of other girls, all with bellies of different sizes. Beds line the walls. Each bed has a night table. One girl leans against her pillows, reading. The rest sit, legs dangling. Bored.

I am definitely not in that room.

"I'm Emily," Elaine says to the girls. She turns and talks directly to the audience: "I'm keeping the same first initial. It's easier to remember than, say, Roberta. After all, I could wake up in the middle of the night wondering, did I pick Rachel, Regina, or Roberta? Emily's better."

A short girl, big belly, turns to the audience: "I used to be Sylvia, but I always hated it. Call me Solange." She faces Emily-Elaine: "Welcome to the baby factory."

Emily-Elaine: "Oh no! Mine's not from an assembly line." She stares at the other girls: "Don't you want to keep your babies?"

A hoody-looking girl with a boy's slick ducktail haircut: "Listen, sweetie, you pop 'em, they take 'em!" She turns to the audience: "I'm Toni ex-Theresa." She turns back to Emily-Elaine: "Hell, it's better that way. If you keep the kid, they'll call him a bastard. Besides, no way you can have it without a husband." Her lips twist into a smile. "You need him, I guess, to help change diapers."

Solange-Sylvia giggles: "Like he ever would." Then her face crumbles: "It's hard, though, when you feel the kicks."

Emily-Elaine gently rubs her belly: I don't feel him yet.

Me and Arthur Miller.

26.

Grandma was home, and the teakettle was whistling.

"Jaimele?"

"Yeah, Grandma, it's me."

Not today, Grandma, please don't ask me about my day.

"So, tea?" She stood, rocking slightly on her heels. That's when I always hug her. I did, but I so didn't want to talk.

I threw my jacket onto the couch and we headed for her room, me carrying the tray with the teapot, cups, sugar for her, two cookies for me.

She sat in her rocker and asked, "So how was your day?"

"*Oy vey*," I said. It was one of the few Yiddish expressions I knew.

"Your accent is better than your father's."

"Mom's Jewish, not Dad. Besides, he's an atheist, Grandma."

"Since when do you have to *daven* to talk Yiddish? When you *daven*, you pray. You laugh, you cry, you argue—it's Yiddish. You think God cares, so long as you can say '*oy vey*'?"

She always made me feel good. I went over and kissed her. "Grandma, when I move out will you come live with me?"

"I should live so long."

That is so my grandma.

"Jamie," she said, clearing her throat. "Sit down. I want to talk to you."

Sometimes if I ask Grandma something, she tells me a story about the old country, and I'm tapping my fingers inside my pockets, waiting for her to get to my question. Then suddenly the story turns out to be exactly what I wanted to know. One thing, though, she has never started with "I want to talk to you."

I sat down.

"I want to talk—"

Stevie burst into the room, waving a paper. "I got the top mark on my English paper, Grandma! And it's 'cause of you!"

She reached out to him. "An English expert I am, you see!"

"We were having a private talk," I said to Stevie, "in case you didn't notice."

Grandma's arm was around him. He wasn't going to leave anytime soon.

"Jealous!"

"Don't be stupid."

"*Kinder*, please!"

"I'm not a child, Grandma," I said.

If she only knew.

"So sorry, your Highness." Stevie gave a deep bow. "Ask her, Grandma, about her boyfriend Paul. He calls her 'Hot Lips Jamie'!"

"You liar!" I swung at him.

Grandma started poking her hairpins.

"Shut up," I said to Stevie. "Can't you see Grandma's upset?"

He leaned against the rocker. I sat down.

No more hairpin poking. Grandma folded her hands in her lap. "It is not upset I am. Just you should know"—Grandma looked right at me—"I want you to know you can always talk with me."

"See," Stevie turned to me, "she's not upset."

"Forever dumb," I said.

Grandma held her arms out. "Come." We stood on both sides of her, pressed in tight. She smelled warm, like mashed potatoes.

Stevie lasted maybe thirty seconds. "I got homework," he said, and bolted.

"I'm a mess, Grandma."

Her arm was still around me. "I have loved you from the moment you were born. When you want, we talk. That's all I wanted to say to you."

I sat back down on the floor, facing her. She rocked slowly. And I, too, rocked back and forth.

27.

Paul knew. Not about being maybe pg, but about—That Night. He and Lois and Elaine. Paul had hugged me. Lois should have done something. Elaine, hopeless.

I sat in the *Record* office. My article was due, but I hadn't been able to write the lede.

Paul stood in front of me. I hadn't heard the door open. I looked at him. "Last year did you see *I'll Cry Tomorrow*, with Susan Hayward?" I said.

He didn't move. He waited. I could wait too.

"Jamie, what's going on?"

I pushed my chair back. It fell over and I walked to the window. What do I say? I'm maybe like Elaine. She's crazy. Maybe I am. Everything's falling apart. I gripped the windowsill.

Paul rushed over and reached out as if trying to stop something.

"Don't worry, I'm not going to jump." I leaned against the radiator and tried to smile.

He looked worried. "Jamie, that's not fair. Talk to me." He gripped my arms.

"Not fair? You . . . you . . . what do you know!" I punched his chest. "Leave me alone! Go away! Forget your stupid article! I quit! Let go! Let me go!" I yelled and shook. I did not want to cry. Me and Susan Hayward.

Paul pulled me close and held me tight. "For what it's worth, I don't accept your resignation."

I pulled away.

He led me back to the chairs and steered me into one. "Talk to me."

Simple as that. Talk to me.

"It's not simple."

We sat, silent, right through the first bell. No way I was going to trig. Paul could go if he wanted.

"I'll tell Mr. Morabito we need a pass," he said. "We've got a hot report to file. He's good that way. Wait here, I'll be right back." He left.

I couldn't have moved anyway.

When he came back, I said, "There is something else."

He put down the two passes, pushed aside the calendar, and sat on the front desk, hands folded in his lap.

"I need someone to go with me to the doctor."

I couldn't look at him. I couldn't breathe.

"Doctor?"

I didn't say anything.

"Jamie," his voice was grave, "you're not saying . . . I mean, you don't think you're . . ."

I heard him get off the desk and come over to where I was sitting.

"Don't touch me, please don't touch me!" I focused on the floor. "I have to get tested, and I have to say I'm married."

I don't remember what else I said. It wasn't a lot, except that I had to make an appointment for the test with the doctor Aunt Sheila told me about.

He pushed a chair next to mine. "Your aunt is a special lady."

"I know."

We sat like that for a while, and then he said he'd come with me.

28.

I was at the front door of the library as fast as I could get there after school let out. I tapped the bell at the front desk, and Mrs. Finley came out of the back office.

"Ah, Jamie Morse. I haven't seen you in a while. How are you?"

I immediately change the subject when someone says, "How are you?"

I nodded and tried to smile while pointing to the re-source shelf behind the desk, "May I have the *Readers' Guide to Periodical Literature*?"

The funny thing is, Mrs. Finley was one of the few people I talked to when Dad was named and arrested. She couldn't have been more decent, and it wasn't because she agreed with all of Dad's politics. She was very clear about that, but said she believed in the Constitution and free speech. "Self-evident" were her words. Mrs. Finley actually hugged me once. It was like sinking into a feather pillow, wrapped in safety.

She can still snap, of course, but she knows her library stuff, that's for sure. You don't see the pillow side of her a lot. Not unless you're in trouble. I am in trouble, but with this kind, who knows what she would say. I couldn't stand her looking at me with "for shame!" written all over her face.

"I've got to find material on Khrushchev's secret speech," I said. "I'm covering it for the *Record*."

"Ah, the denunciation of Stalin. Interesting." Her lips pursed.

"They say he talked for four hours," I said, "about how Stalin had made himself into a superman. They called it something I can't remember."

"The cult of personality. And," Mrs. Finley added, "Chairman Khrushchev detailed the crimes Stalin had committed." She tapped her pencil on the volume. "The speech was in late February, I believe. You'll likely find material starting this past March."

The heavy red volume was an old friend. I had pored through it looking for articles on Senator McCarthy, the Hollywood Ten, and other stories about the government and the movie industry hunting down "Reds" the way they'd hunted down Dad.

I lugged the book over to a table in the back and spread out my papers. Mrs. Finley was busy with a line of people at the front desk. I was glad. I didn't want her to see what else I was checking. I mean, what if the doctor tells me I really am. . . .

I opened the volume to A. Abortion. "The Abortion Racket: Product of Laggard Law." *The Nation* magazine. I found the bound volume of *Nation* magazines and brought it to the table. In New York City, according to the district attorney, when you called one of these doctors who would do it, you first talked about pairs of nylons. *Nylons! Like some ladies store?* Six pairs meant you were six weeks pg, eight meant eight. It's an Underground Railroad, with codes, conductors, stationmasters! I shut the book. You have to know somebody who could tell you the code. But first you have to know somebody to tell you about somebody. I began to sweat.

Mrs. Finley came out from behind the front desk. I quickly opened to K and scribbled on my pad. She was coming toward me.

"Found some stuff," I said. I closed the book and covered my notes, but she hadn't heard me. She had turned down an aisle well before my table. A young kid followed her.

I needed a break. I got up and looked through the pile of newspapers Mrs. Finley keeps in the reading area.

I do think there is a god and he's out to punish me. Yesterday's *Daily News*, front page, picture of two cops holding a man's hands behind his back. It's nighttime. Headline: ABORTION RING SMASHED. Six doctors in Queens arrested.

Who told on them? The *N.Y. Post* front page for the same day was

COPS SHUT
VICE HOUSE

At the end of the story on the inside page was a box: TWO SENTENCED IN FATAL ABORTION. The woman who died was from Brooklyn, but the two people were sentenced in Bronx County Court to prison terms of twelve and a half to twenty-five years. Everybody travels. Aunt Sheila's person is in Brooklyn. My head was spinning. Maybe Elaine was doing the right thing.

I opened to the A index again in the *Readers' Guide*. Adoption. *LIFE* magazine ran an article in the February 19, 1951, issue called "The Adoption of Linda Joy."

The volumes were on the bottom shelf in the research section. I brought 1951 to my table. Pages 99 to 105. Five small pictures at the beginning. The caption said, "Unwed mother of eighteen." The pregnant girl arrives at a place like where Elaine's going. She tells the social worker "Okay she's yours to give away." After birth, there's a pic of the nurse holding the baby, and then the girl says goodbye and watches the social worker walk off. Not a problem. The girl says she has "a long life ahead of me," and that "it hurts, but . . ." After all, the article says, there's a real shortage of babies available for adoption. The main part of the article with big pics is about this wonderful couple, of whom there are at least a million who can't have a kid and want to adopt, so says the writer. The unwed mother is doing a public service. Two words only, "It hurts," and that's in a caption you could easily miss.

"A different article?" Mrs. Finley stood next to the table.

"I . . . we . . ."

"We are in the midst of a clean-up-the-city campaign," she said, pointing to VICE HOUSE headline. "Like Prohibition, when something is criminalized, it goes underground, and that is often more dangerous than what has been deemed unlawful."

The thing about Mrs. Finley is if you stick it out to the end of her very long sentences, she makes you think.

"The human species has a great deal to answer for," she said. She whipped out the handkerchief she has in the cuff of her sleeve and gave a Finley sniff. In a flash I realized that's how she punctuates. An exclamation sniff!

Mrs. Finley tucked the handkerchief back in her sleeve. "What is your storyline?"

When she wants, her sentences can be short and to the point.

I sat, paralyzed.

"Well," she said, with a very small sniff that apparently didn't need the handkerchief. She waited. "The connection to your school? Why is your school newspaper concerned about so-called dens of vice?"

Elaine had said, "If I'd do it, it meant I loved him." That's what Neil had told her. I was forced, love had nothing to do with it, and both of us were trapped.

"Mrs. Finley," I said looking down at the paper, "some girls get in trouble." I couldn't breathe. I couldn't look at her.

Go away, please.

This time it was a kind god. A young girl tapped Mrs. Finley on the arm. "I need help," she said. Mrs. Finley left.

Me too.

29.

I don't have enough hair for a French twist. I tried to make a pageboy, but my hair's way too curly to look good. I had binged at Woolworth's: a new lipstick, rouge, and a powder compact. I still had Lois's eyeliner, and I didn't poke myself this time.

Paul said he'd gotten a ring from Woolworth's. We met in front of the doctor's building, where he almost walked by me, then did a classic double take. It was for real, because Paul is a lousy actor. I told him he didn't have to say anything, only pretend he's my husband.

I took his arm. "All right, Mr. DeMille, I'm ready for my closeup."

He jerked away from me. "For Pete's sake, Jamie, this is not a movie. It's real."

"You think I don't know that? Today is a big scene for me. I'm just trying to get—"

"Get what? You want a medical test. That's it. The less you lie, the less you have to remember, the fewer mistakes."

Why did he always have to be right?

The doctor's office had a potted fern in the corner. Ferns stay the same, green and healthy looking. A flower pot would be a big mistake. Forget a couple of times to water, forget once to lop off the head of the dead flower, and it's people crying in the waiting room. Ferns don't make you cry.

Paul walked over to the magazine rack, and I went to the reception desk. "Jamie Morse. I have an appointment."

"Please have a seat, I'll call you in a moment."

Paul came back from the rack empty-handed. No wonder: *Good Housekeeping, Better Homes and Gardens, Woman's Day, Cosmopolitan*. There was a *LIFE* magazine on the table next to me, and I handed it to him.

I wanted to look like a reader of one of those other magazines, but I'd never read one. I turned the ring on my finger. Left hand, I'd told Paul, is if you're married. The ring was a little loose, but not enough to slip off.

"Mrs. Morse?"

Paul looked at me. I whispered, "I used my name."

At the desk the receptionist handed me a clipboard. "I'm here for the test to see if I'm . . ."

"Of course you are, dear." Smile. "Fill this out and bring it back to me." Smile.

The easy stuff, name, date of birth (I made it two years earlier), address, allergies, hospitalizations. Date of last menstruation. I caught my breath. Of course they wanted to know that. Why was I surprised?

Paul read. I counted the squares of linoleum, right to left, left to right, up and down, down and up.

"Peterson." A man and woman followed the nurse into a back room.

Ten minutes later, "Liebman." Another couple disappeared beyond the green door.

"Morse." Finally.

Paul stood up with me. "I'm Paul Morse, remember?"

"You can wait here Mr. Morse. She won't be long."

The nurse closed the door behind me and gave me a sharp look. I felt like a kid dressed up in my mother's clothes. She handed me a cup and test tube. "The bathroom is the second door on the left. Fill the tube and bring it here." She pointed to a desk with trays and files.

I put the tube and cup on the ledge below the bathroom mirror and took the ring off. I was terrified I'd pee on my hand. You've got to get the cup in exactly the right place. The last thing I needed was to have to fish out this cheap ring. I felt nauseous. Not from being maybe pregnant, but from the grossness of it all.

The nurse had labels ready when I brought out the tube.

"The results will be back in two weeks."

"That long?"

She never looked up. Just like Nurse Barclay at school. "You can try calling in ten days."

The receptionist was a hundred and eighty degrees the opposite. She held up crossed fingers on both hands, beamed, and leaned forward conspiratorially. "Let's hope there's a little one in the basket!"

Paul gripped my arm, smiled back at her, and said, "Thank you." I felt weak in the knees.

We went to lunch. He was starved. All I wanted was a chocolate egg cream and french fries.

"Hey, listen, maybe you're not," he said between mouthfuls.

Maybe I'm not. Or maybe there'll be two more weeks of getting bigger.

JUNE

30.

I can't button my skirt.

31.

This cannot be happening to me.

I dropped my books on the bed and circled the room. I'm wearing out the rug. Mom's at work, Dad's looking for work, Stevie's at band practice, and Grandma's gone shopping. It's me and Scruffy.

I looked into the mirror on my bureau. It was dark, but I didn't turn on the desk lamp.

At some point, you're alone.

Pregnant!

A little push against my leg. Me and Scruffy.

I stared at myself. "Maybe it'll work." I frowned. "It has to." I don't have a second floor in a house like the girl Carol told us about, just an apartment stairwell. I kept talking. "Fourteen steps with a landing turn in the middle. A problem," I said to the mirror. "Difficult, requiring a swivel."

I took time changing clothes. I hung up my skirt and blouse and folded my sweater. Third drawer from the top. This sweater was the only neat thing in there. I have thick and thin dungarees. The thick ones are a little looser. That'll be good. I pulled out a T-shirt and blouse. Scruffy jumped on the pile. "I'll be back," I said as I lifted him off. "Wait for me." Socks and penny loafers. They slide better than my Keds.

You've got to be a careful planner for something like this.

I have just enough hair for a small ponytail, and I didn't pin the few pieces on the sides that weren't long enough. Better not to use bobby pins at a time like this.

What else? No cookies. Nothing in the stomach. Don't want to be sick. Not that way.

What else? Better take a light jacket so it looks like I meant to go someplace. It's not cold enough for gloves. Too bad.

What else? I looked around my room. Everything seemed normal. I rearranged the two small pillows on the bed. Then I put them back again in their original places.

It's time.

We have the same Van Gogh bridge picture as Aunt Sheila and Uncle George. Ours is in the living room over the table. We don't have those brown, dead-looking sunflowers.

I took my key, left the apartment, went past the elevator, and opened the door to the stairwell. I didn't let it slam. I was walking through thick custard.

Tight focus on ponytail. Camera pulls back and widens at slight angle. The Girl is in full frame. Left hand on stairwell banister. Both arms reach up to cover head. Every move in slow motion. The Girl stands rigid. Three seconds that seem an eternity. Dissolve to close-up on face. Eyes squeezed shut, mouth slightly open. A jerk upward, and face is out of frame. Crashing/ tumbling sound. Pull back to wide-angle, a move- ment blur. Camera shakes. The Girl's hand tries to grasp banister, misses. Soft focus of roll on landing. Sharp beats. Focus. Body careens down second set of stairs. The Girl's head and chest on landing bottom, legs twisted upward on stairs.

I lay trembling. I'd scraped my cheek with a fingernail when I grabbed for the banister. I hadn't wanted to break the fall, but instinct took over. My back ached. I inched my legs down and lay with my knees pulled up to my chest. Is anything broken? I tested each arm and leg. Everything moved. No sharp pains. Fierce aches. I touched my face lightly and looked at my fingers. A little blood from my cheek. Nothing else. I looked between my legs. *Why isn't anything coming out of me?* That was the whole point.

THAT WAS THE WHOLE POINT!

I rolled over onto my knees. I wasn't sure I could stand. I fell back on my side. I'd failed, and now I couldn't

159

even get up. Again I rolled onto my knees. I crawled over to the banister and pulled myself up. My arm wailed in the shoulder socket. Every part of me, every cell, screamed. If you multiplied the worst charley horse you've ever had by ten thousand, that gets close.

It took minutes to get the key out of my pocket. The back of my hand was scraped. No blood, just raw skin. Inside the apartment I lowered my dungarees. One knee was bleeding, but not enough to have soaked through the pants.

What now?

Vodka and 7-UP! Isn't that what Lois's friend had said? My dungarees were at my ankles. I pulled them up. It took an hour.

Nobody's a big drinker in this family, not counting Uncle George, but his bottle collection is not here. Mom and Dad have only a few. They fit in the narrow bottom cabinet next to the kitchen pipe. It took several attempts at bending to pull out the vodka bottle. I rested after I lifted it up to the counter. Please, *please* let there be 7-UP.

Of course not. Mom doesn't believe in sodas. Can't anything go right? Seltzer?

The thing that fools you is that vodka looks like water and it doesn't have much of a smell. Did my nose get banged on the stairs? Does it usually have a strong smell?

I took a tall glass from the dish rack and filled it, three-quarters vodka, one-quarter seltzer. I waited for the bubbles to calm down. If I didn't, I'd hiccup for the next ten minutes, and my ribs hurt too much for that.

Maybe I should bring the glass into my room, so if anything happens I'd be next to my bed. Please, let something happen!

I don't remember anything after I sat down on the bed and began to drink.

The faintest of echoes down a long tunnel. As the sound came closer, it careened off the tunnel walls. Smother it! I tried to turn, to hide.

"Jamie! Wake up!"

I squinted. The light was like a nail across a blackboard. I think I saw a cheek. Stevie. His face was right up against mine. Still it was a blur.

"Go away," I croaked.

"Mom said to get you. Dinner." The blur moved away. "Duty done," it said.

My eyes closed, but I heard him leave.

"What have you done?" Mom stood by my bed. "Get up this minute!"

It hurt to look up. It hurt to move. I tried.

"I can't."

Her face was close to mine. "Pete! Come in here! Quick!" Footsteps. "Do you smell that? She's drunk!"

I felt an arm under my shoulders. I didn't know what hurt more, my head, my back, my shoulders. My heart. Dad propped me up and sat next to me. I tipped into him. Mom sat down on the other side.

"Why?" she said, her voice now soft.

Maybe the vodka will work. I have to wait.

"Cramps."

She sighed. "I'm so relieved."

Dad was incredulous. "She's drunk and in pain and you're relieved?"

"You can never understand what cramps are like. Go," she said. "Get everything on the table. I'll be right in."

She sat holding me. I didn't tell her I hurt all over, and she didn't notice my scraped cheek. Everybody believes cramps. I would. I'm grateful for them. I wish I had them.

32.

The next morning Mom called the principal's office and told them I was sick. Then everyone left. I went into the bathroom and jumped up and down at least a hundred times. Nothing came out. Nothing, and believe me I checked.

Maybe it's because I didn't use 7-UP.

I collapsed onto the chair. If this is a hangover, never will another drop pass my lips, lips that are rough, stinging sand. The Vaseline jar was on top of the bureau, a mile away. The telephone rang and a new pain was added, a rasping saw in my head. How does anyone drink if this is the next day?

I stood up, quivering, and groped my way into Grandma's room. The closest phone. It was a toss-up whether at my pace I could make it before the caller hung up.

When I reached the phone, I didn't have the strength to say anything.

"Jamie? Is that you?" Elaine's voice was so piercing, I had to move the phone away from my ear.

"I hope not," I muttered.

She started to cry. At least not loudly. I lay down gingerly on Grandma's bed, cradling the phone between my head and the pillow.

"I'm going tomorrow to a wage home. I'm supposed to help some family. Housework, that sort of thing."

I pushed myself to sit up. "You're going to be a maid?"

Elaine sighed. "You don't know what it's been like here. I'm too big for a girdle. If anyone comes over, I have to stay upstairs. Nobody can see me."

"In the attic? Like Anne Frank listening through floorboards?"

"It's not funny. If they ask about me, my mother says I'm doing homework or I have a cold. I haven't seen anyone in over a month."

I touched my stomach. How big before they hide me?

"The worst is the car. When we go to the doctor, I practically crawl to the driveway and then I have to lie down on the back seat. I stayed in the car when my mom bought smock dresses. They are so ugly. And after tomorrow they're going to tell people I'm helping with my aunt who's sick. I'll write to you," she said. "They don't have room yet in the Catholic Home, that's why. But they will soon." She paused, and said, "and you could come."

"One preggers goes on visiting day to say hello to another." I tried to laugh, but it came out a snort.

"Come stay there. With me," she said urgently.

"So Neil can take me away too?"

She hung up.

Why did I do that? Stevie's right, I have turned mean.

The phone rang again, and I grabbed it.

"Elaine? I'm sorry. I didn't mean it. Really I didn't."

Silence.

"Hello?" I said.

"What didn't you mean?"

"Mom! It's nothing. Me and Elaine, you know, we had a fight. Really it's nothing."

I could hear her moving papers. "I wanted to check on how you're doing," she said. "You were pretty miserable last night, and I imagine your head feels like a cracked coconut this morning."

"I'm not seeing double anymore."

I could almost hear a slight smile. "I want you to take the pot roast out of the refrigerator," she said. "Put it in the oven at 300 degrees. I'll be home in a little over an hour."

Mom's okay that way. No heavy moral laid on, but believe me, you get the idea.

I dialed Elaine. I couldn't leave it like that. She answered on the first ring.

"Neil?"

"It's me."

"Oh."

"Listen, I didn't mean it. I'm trying to work things out here. You know. About me. And it's hard. So I'm really sorry."

I waited.

"If that's an apology, I accept it." And then she said, "It's your choice."

I swallowed hard. "You're my oldest friend." As I said it I knew nothing would ever be the same. Ever.

33.

The caf was half full. Georgina saw me and waved.

"Carol and Kay are still at that citywide Latin competition." She looked hard at me. "You into muumuus now?"

"Yeah. I think the colors are great." I looked down at the print. Why do they have to make them so loud?

"I thought you said you didn't like green on you?"

If this keeps up, she'll figure it out. I know Georgina. "It's red and green together."

She laughed, "Christmas in springtime."

And a little present on the way. Oh god.

Georgina picked the celery out of the tuna fish in her sandwich.

"It's a good thing we're friends," I said, getting away from muumuus. "Somebody else might think that's gross."

She leaned towards me. "What's gross is your not

saying anything. You think I haven't noticed? What is *not* gross is that I haven't said anything to Kay and Carol."

I looked down at my own tuna sandwich. The smell was overwhelming, and I began to cough. Georgina pushed a glass of water towards me.

"Dry throat," I croaked.

She leaned back, folded her arms and said, "So?"

"It's awful."

"Paul?"

"Never!" I pushed the sandwich as far from me as I could, and blew my nose. "It was . . . horrible. I can't talk about it."

She came over to my side of the table. "What are you going to do?"

I grabbed her hand. "I have to make a phone call. Come with me?"

Georgina put my tray on top of hers, and we left the caf. The *Record* office was empty, as I knew it would be. I sat at the front desk, and Georgina pulled up a chair. I picked at the blotter like a scab.

I took out the piece of paper from Aunt Sheila. There was no doubt in my mind, but I called the doctor's office anyway.

"This is . . . Mrs. Morse."

Georgina mouthed "Mrs.?"

"Just a moment please." The receptionist put down the phone and then came back chirping. "Good news! You are definitely pregnant."

I don't know why it struck like a cannonball. I'd known it, but now . . . now it was absolute.

"Jamie, who was that?"

"Good news," I said, holding back a scream. "I'm definitely—"

Georgina got up and walked to the back of the room. She stood for a moment facing the windows, then walked back to the front. "What are you going to do?"

"I don't know."

"Do you want to have it?"

"I can't do that. I can't!" My head was like a metronome that wouldn't stop swinging from side to side. "I can't go through that, nine months inside me, and then give it away. I can't."

We sat not talking.

My hands were ice cold. Georgina had her hand on my arm. Hers was warm.

"If I find someone, you'll come with me?"

She looked scared. She nodded.

34.

Why do I have to be so ordinary? Morning sickness, and it's nasty enough to come late some days. Like today. I hate to throw up; it leaves such an awful taste. I've been eating saltine crackers like there's no tomorrow. What's really awful is this strange rash on my left cheek. It's lucky I bought that powder-puff compact. Kay said to me the other day that I looked like a painted woman. But she immediately started talking about something else. Almost everyone has some pimples, so it's not a big surprise. But these are not pimples.

"Hey, Miss Hot Lips, letters." Stevie charged in from my doorway, leapt up and tossed envelopes onto the chair. "Practicing my hook shot, not bad!" He whirled out. I was too tired to work up anger.

Letters. Who'd be writing me? The top one had Lois's return address.

Dear Jamie,

I've thought a lot about what you said and you're right. I shouldn't have let it happen. I should have thought of you as my kid sister, not a young friend. That's not an excuse, I know. It's just what I've been thinking about. And I'll never forgive myself for letting you down so badly.

I want you to know that I gave Jonas what for. He said you'd told him you were eighteen, not that that makes it okay. Then he said he'd pulled out. I told him he was an absolute bastard and I never want to see him again.

I am so sorry this happened to you. It would be awful for anyone, but to me you are special, which makes it particularly awful. I hope you know I care deeply about you.

Love,

Lois

P.S. I understand why you haven't answered my calls, but if you can forgive me and there's anything I can do—*please* call.

I crumpled the paper, but then flattened it out and put it in the second drawer of my desk between two pads. I put the dictionary on top of it. It belonged with a pile of words. I couldn't help it. I was still angry. She should have watched out for me.

The next two envelopes were from Elaine. The first letter was scribbled on a torn sheet of notebook paper. She wrote it from the wage home.

> I've got my own room in the basement, but they let
> me watch television in their living room if no one is
> visiting. I've been washing a lot of dishes. They have a
> baby who screams through half the night. Mine won't,
> I know. He'll be adorable like Neil. I wrote Neil for a
> picture to put in my locket. It hasn't come yet.

A no-crying baby. Sure, like Neil will send a picture, like
her parents will let her marry Neil.

The second letter had a different return address and a
folded envelope inside along with her letter.

> I'm here at last. It's not so bad. You were right about
> the name thing, though. I'm Eleanor!

I was close with Emily.

The nuns, she said, had them busy every minute.
Up at 6:30, breakfast over by 7:00, lunch at noon, different classes each day, mostly girl-getting-ready-to-be-
mother things like sewing, knitting, putting together a
layette, which she said was sad, since everything would
be left for the family that's adopting. Except, of course,
she says, for Neil Jr's. things, which she'll take when
they get married. And every Friday there was a medical
checkup.

The rest was pretty depressing, although I don't know
if Elaine meant it that way.

Sister Francis Catherine is kind. She tries to make us feel good about what we're doing by telling us there's a good Catholic family waiting for the baby. The social worker who comes once a week says the same thing. She had us write on one side of a page what that family would give the baby. On the other side we wrote what we could give. I don't care that they have lots of money and a big house and good schools and that Neil and I won't start with much. I wrote I have lots and lots and lots of LOVE!!! NOBODY could give my baby as much love as me.

You're my best friend. You have to do this for me. I'm not allowed to write to Neil. So I'm sending you the letter to mail for me. PLEASE! He can't come for me if he doesn't know where I am. You have to HELP!!!

The folded envelope was addressed to Neil. And there was more.

Margaret (her real name is Pat) is like me. She's going to keep her baby. She won't talk to the social worker anymore. Maybe I won't either.

I started a letter to Elaine. I told her a little about me and the test, but nothing else. I wanted to say, what if Neil doesn't come through? But I didn't.

35.

That doctor in Pennsylvania—Stevens? Smith? What was his name! Stupid, stupid stupid! Why hadn't I put that piece of paper in a safe place?

What was I wearing at Lois's? The grey slacks. I dug into each pocket as if by magic it would appear. What blouse? The striped one, but it had no pockets. Someplace in my wallet. No paper. I emptied my bag on the bed. A crumpled note from Paul about the ring. Tissues. Clean. Used. The compact, lipstick, pencils. Carol's notes from Mr. Morabito's last class. There! Bottom corner of the bag where the lint lives.

Spencer! That's it, Dr. Spencer, and Lois had written what to say: vaginal discharge.

My hand shook. Could I say those words? I shoved everything back in the bag, grabbed a sweater and left.

Grandma sat in the rocker reading.

"Be back soon." I left before I changed my mind.

The phone booth by Mrs. Manny's candy store was empty. How much money did I need to call Pennsylvania? Mrs. Manny didn't smile much, but she liked me.

She looked up in surprise. "Your father, he picked up the paper this morning."

"It's me. I need candy today," I said and held up the Almond Joy and Hershey bars I'd taken from the rack. I pocketed the change she gave me.

Outside, I dialed the operator. I pictured her in a long line of operators sitting in front of a gigantic telephone board, shoving phone jacks into little holes, pulling them out, crossing wires, uncrossing them—millions of connections traveling overhead along telephone wires from pole to pole all the way from New York City to Ashland, PA.

"I want to call Pennsylvania."

"You can dial that directly now."

I held the phone, bewildered. I had to do this alone?

The phone in Ashland rang. Fifteen times. I must have dialed the wrong number. I hung up and tried again. Twenty-seven rings. Then I remembered Lois had said the police warned Dr. Spencer before a raid, and he'd shut down for a while.

This couldn't be happening.

It's getting close to three months. Would I run out of time?

I didn't stay long at Aunt Sheila's. You don't have to. She doesn't ask a lot of questions. I told her a friend in college had missed her period and was . . . you know. The college part was important. I didn't want her asking how old she was.

"That name you said. The lady in Brooklyn?"

The flashing knitting needles were still for a moment. "If you're asking me for help," she said, knitting again and looking at me without missing a stitch, "I assume your friend can't go to her mother's doctor."

Aunt Sheila is smarter than you might think. She wrote down a name on a piece of paper. "Your friend, she's eighteen, I assume. She has to be." Aunt Sheila folded the paper and handed it to me.

I love my Aunt Sheila.

I don't dream much. Everybody says you dream all the time, but if I do, I don't remember. That night I dreamt and remembered.

I was in a city. Tall buildings lined the streets, tilting in like trees in a savage storm. I turned corners. Sometimes I ran. I clutched a small brown paper bag. I held the bag in front of me. People walked past me without looking. The streets turned into hallways, long corridors. I opened doors and held up the bag. The doors closed. Nobody would take the bag.

I woke up with my pajamas sweat-soaked.

36.

I was behind Georgina on the cafeteria line. I had to make sure she would come with me.

"You really want to do this?" she said.

"Absolutely." I tried to sound a hundred percent confident, but my voice cracked. I was terrified. *Did* I want this? Was it right? What if I died? Like that lady in the newspaper in Brooklyn, which is where I'm going.

"It's tonight at 6:30," I said. "Meet me at 5:00 by the subway at Castle Hill?"

She mouthed yes as Kay joined us. All I ate was mashed potatoes. I'm ravenous, but everything else was too awful to consider.

Grandma was in bed when I came home from school. She looked tiny with only her head and arms above the quilt.

"Would you like me to open the window?"

She patted the quilt. "I'm napping, that's all. Come, sit."

"Some tea? I can make some tea? A danish? A cracker?"

Her eyes grew soft. "Jaimele, something is happening with you. Tell me."

Without thinking, I touched my cheek, the side with the rash. Grandma reached up and took my hand.

"Trouble?" she said.

"Oh, Grandma," I curled by her side, my head on her shoulder. "I don't know what to do."

"It's you, not just your friend, yes?"

I sat up. "I want to graduate and go to college." She stroked my arm. I told her but didn't say who or when it happened or about tonight.

She listened without saying anything. Her long grey hair was draped over each shoulder. There were no hairpins to poke. They lay in a pile on the bedside table.

"Your mama, have you talked with her?" There was no judgment in her voice, just a question.

"I will. Later. I want first—"

"She will help."

I shook my head. "It's me, Grandma. Me, and I'm . . ."

How do I tell her I'm so scared and I don't want to be talked into anything or out of anything and I don't know for sure what they'll say?

"I gotta go now." I bent down and kissed her dry cheek.

Georgina was waiting for me. I showed her the address Aunt Sheila had written, and we climbed the stairs to the subway platform. I have no idea if the train came right away or we had to wait. We were on, and I was grateful for the rumble as we moved, the screech when we stopped, the whistle as the train started up again, the sliding *whoosh* of the doors—all the noises blocked out everything. Except the pit in my stomach. That stayed and grew. The train tilted around curves, and suddenly we were plunged into darkness as we went from the overhead track down into the underground subway tunnels.

"When is a subway not a subway?" Georgina said. She didn't expect an answer. We hardly ever called it the El, and never the Elevated. You just said subway. We barreled on into Brooklyn and came up into the air again.

On the street I showed the address to a woman pushing a baby carriage. She pointed ahead. "Make a right at the corner, then the second left, three blocks down and you'll cross Rose Hill. Keep walking. You'll find it."

"Don't say a word," I said to Georgina as we walked toward the corner. "I don't want to hear anything about roses or hills."

"I wasn't thinking anything like that," she said.

"I'm sorry. I'm just . . ."

"Hey, it's okay. So what does this lady know about me?"

"I didn't tell her anything."

The black pit inside me was getting bigger. I stopped and leaned against a lamppost.

"You scared?" she said.

I was sweating.

"If you want," she took a deep breath, "when she . . . you know, does it, I'll hold your hand."

That was major for Georgina. She'd been excused from dissecting the frog last year in biology. Couldn't stand cutting into flesh.

I squeezed her hand. She was a true friend.

"Just don't tell anybody," I said.

She looked appalled that I could even think she might.

A really true friend.

Past Rose Hill the house numbers were going down, so we were headed in the right direction. We stopped in front of a little grey house with green trim. Georgina opened the gate of the low fence, and we walked toward the front steps. I started counting. Eight steps from the gate to the stoop. Five steps up. Two steps to the door. Two rings on the bell.

I think the lady who opened the door was normal-looking, but I couldn't swear to it. I couldn't swear to anything. Her voice sounded like it came from across the ocean. We went in, and Georgina asked if she could use the bathroom. The lady pointed down the hallway, "Second door on the right." Then she began to ask me questions, but she didn't write anything down. And she never asked me about my husband, even though I wore the ring. She did ask where I lived, and said she had a sister in the Bronx.

"On the phone you said you were eighteen. Is that right?" she asked.

"Eighteen, yes."

Georgina came back and sat in one of the chairs next to a table with magazines. The lady turned to her. "Are you a relative?"

Georgina closed the magazine. "A cousin."

"And how old are you?"

Georgina smiled. "Same birthday," she nodded toward me. "March 3, 1940."

The lady's face twisted in shock. She stepped back. "1940!" and then everything turned upside down.

"I'm sorry you came all the way."

She steered us out and shut the door. The lock turned.

I slumped down on the stoop. My ears filled with a ferocious pounding. I held my head to try to stop it.

"What happened?" Georgina sat down next to me.

I couldn't look at her. "You've ruined it. I told her I was eighteen." My voice was flat. I had nothing left.

Georgina gasped. Then she took my arm and led me to the subway.

37.

It was late when I got home. They were all in the living room. Grandma in the rocker, Dad half-asleep in his chair, Mom on one end of the couch, plus two uncles and an aunt. Stevie must have been in his room.

"My, you look down," Mom said.

Grandma leaned a little forward, her eyes questioning. I looked away.

"Hey, kid, what's up?" Uncle Maury folded the newspaper and smiled at me.

Last night I had another dream. I was up a tree, out on a limb, with a saw. *I was sawing between me and the tree trunk*. What do I say? "I'm fine, Uncle Maury. I'm up a tree."

"Tell them, Jamie." Grandma's voice was barely above a whisper, but every head turned first to her and then to me.

Nobody said a word, but booming through the room was "Tell us what?" They thought in one voice.

I weighed five hundred pounds, too tired to walk away. Too tired to stand. I leaned against the table. Nothing I'd tried had worked. Paul had come with me. Georgina had come with me. But in the end it was me, alone. Nothing had worked. I saw them sitting there. The closest people in the world to me, and strangers.

What did I know about them? Mom loves me, but she's busy working. Dad, he loves me too, but he's busy job-hunting, and he's not all himself. Uncle Maury loves me, but he thinks I'm smart because I say the right thing on a questionnaire. Not fair? I'm not fair. I don't want to be fair. I want something to make this right.

And Grandma, she ... she loves me, period. I went over to the rocker and sat down on the rug next to her. She reached down and took my hand. "Tell them," she said again.

"How?" I really wanted to know. "How?"

"Tell them."

I did. I don't remember where I started, and I know it was mixed up and out of order, but everybody listened, not a single interruption. "This guy," I said, "he was Lois's friend, and we went to a party—not Lois, just me and him—and I drank wine and we went to a restaurant and he took me to his apartment and I shouldn't have gone but I thought he was just going to kiss me ..." I started to cry.

Grandma saved me. "Advantage he took, he violated!"

Aunt Sheila's hand flew to her mouth. Dad closed his eyes, and Mom reached out to touch me.

The next part was hardest. "I missed my period."

Great timing—Stevie came in, and Mom motioned him to go back.

"I need a glass of water," he said. "What's going on?"

Dad looked at him over his glasses, and Stevie went into the kitchen. Nobody said anything until he was back in his room, and we heard his door close. I knew he probably opened it again and was listening. That's what we always did when they sent us away. But I didn't have the energy to care.

Dad started. "What do you want, Jamie? Now I'm saying it, what do you *really* want?"

"How does she know what she wants? She's a child."

I was startled. I hadn't expected that from Uncle Maury.

Dad came right back. "She may be a young person, but she has lived sixteen years and knows many things about herself."

Dad!

Uncle Maury kept brushing his hair off his forehead. "Of course. You're right. I only meant we have to help her. Jamie," he appealed to me, "that's what I meant."

Mom fidgeted. She pressed the folds of her dress and started to say something, but stopped. She reached behind her legs to straighten the seams on her nylons. Then she folded her hands in her lap. "If you want to have the child, Jamie," she said, "we will help you."

I stopped breathing.

She went over to Dad's chair and sat on the arm. He nodded, and I knew it wasn't a baby Dad wanted. He wanted his family.

"I love you both," I said, and I meant it. "But I can't. I don't know all of why. It's not just going to college." I touched my belly. "This is not a baby yet, and I can't let it be one. I mean, how could I have a baby and not take care of it?"

Grandma kissed the top of my head.

Mom held out her arms.

"We will figure this out," Dad said.

This is my family.

38.

After lunch I went to the *Record* office. I knew Paul would be there, and I gave him my article. He put it down without looking at it. "You never told me what happened," he said. "Did you call the doctor's office? The test must be back."

He looked sweet and caring. And I felt much older. "It's real," I said. "I called, but I knew it anyway."

He stood up and walked to the windows and back at least three times.

"What are you going to do?"

I turned toward the door.

"Jamie, listen, whatever you decide . . . I mean, whenever . . . I mean . . ."

I looked at him.

". . . you want to go to the movies tomorrow night?"

"Okay," and I left.

The mailbox was full when I got home. Mom's *New Yorker* magazine took up a lot of the space. A couple of envelopes looked like bills. And a letter from Elaine. I hadn't heard from her in a while, and I hadn't written after that last letter. I tore open the envelope. The beginning was a shocker.

Margaret ran away with her baby. She was the one like me who was going to keep it. Well, she gave birth a week ago. There's a separate building here where they keep the babies until they're sent away, and they'll let you visit if you want. Some of the girls don't. They leave as soon as they can. Margaret went every time she could. Last night about 10:30, the lights were already out and suddenly the bells started ringing like crazy. We saw the shadow of the nuns running in the hallway. When they turned on our light, Sister Mary Thomas stood there and wanted to know who of us knew. Everyone looked at me because I was Margaret's closest friend here, but I didn't know. I'm glad for her!

After that, Elaine's handwriting got shaky. "They keep telling me I'm being selfish," she wrote.

I'm so confused. Am I selfish? What do you think? Sister Mary Thomas tells all of us all the time that what we did was shameful and we should be grateful for what they're doing for us here. The social worker said to me who was I to think I could give a baby a good life. "You need a husband for that," she said. I told her I would have one. Did you mail my letter to Neil? He hasn't written. I don't understand it. Maybe he never got it. Will you call him for me? The doctor told me it's going to happen soon. Maybe in a week or sooner. Please will you call? Here's his number . . .

I couldn't bear to read on. Sometimes I think hope is when you don't want to know. I knew. I knew Neil would never come. He hadn't answered her phone calls. Why would he answer her letter? He was a stinking jerk. But deep down a tiny piece of me understood. I didn't want to have a child either. But he should have told her, the stinking rotten jerk.

I wrote her a two-word letter. "I'll call." It wouldn't help, this I knew, but I'd call. There was a deep hole in my chest filled with ache. I never knew before that an ache was something you could put both hands around—it had a shape, a thickness, a weight. Elaine was so frantic about Neil, she couldn't even ask me what was happening with me. Strange, but it didn't make me angry. Just very sad.

Three days later there was another letter. That's too fast. I pulled the first envelope out of the waste basket. Elaine had reversed the numbers of our building. The first one had been mailed over ten days ago. I tore open the second letter. It was very short.

I'm home. They took away my beautiful baby.

39.

I walked from the station to Elaine's house. It wasn't far, just a couple of blocks from the town's main street, Elaine said. All these porches with nobody sitting on them. No rockers. So much for Hollywood.

Elaine's house had a sloping lawn up to her porch. I didn't see a bell, just a knocker. The door opened almost immediately, and Elaine stepped out and gave me a hug.

The kitchen was big and opened onto a small back porch. She offered me coffee, and when I said "Sure," I remembered Paul and tonight's movie date.

"Can I make a quick call?"

She pointed to a phone on the wall. I dialed the *Record* office at school. He's there most Saturdays working on layout. *Please be there alone!* I didn't want Elaine to hear me say his name. When he answered, I said only that I'd have to call later. I might not make it.

I needn't have worried. Elaine was sitting on the back porch, paying no attention to me. She poured the coffee, and we sat and drank.

"I'm drinking again," she said and raised her cup. I couldn't tell if she was angry or resigned. Maybe both. She didn't ask about me, and I didn't say anything. I'd come because she's my friend, but not a two-way sharing friend anymore, at least not now.

"You look tired," I said.

She bit her lip. "They let me see her only once. I don't know where she will be, who'll hold her when she cries, who'll tickle her belly."

"It's a good Catholic fam—"

"Stop it!" And then she said, "I can't cry. I've run out of tears."

We sat for a while, and then there wasn't anything more to say. When I left, my head was spinning. I was desperate to get what I wanted, and so far I hadn't. Elaine had made her choice, but nobody, not Neil, not her parents, not the Home, had listened. What does it mean to choose if you can't get what you want or if nobody listens?

I called Lois from Penn Station. I didn't blame her, I said.

40.

Dad and Mom have a friend who's an obstetrician. They were political friends back before Dad went to prison. He didn't "cross the street," so he's one of the good guys so far as I'm concerned. And he was good to me.

Mom's the one who called him, and she took me to his office. He wanted to talk to me alone, no mother, no nurse. He needed to know when I thought it had happened (it was not a day I'd forget) and when I'd had my last period. But mostly he told me what I should say on the information sheet his nurse would give me. He listed a bunch of symptoms— unusual discharge, excessive bleeding, bad cramping—that kind of thing. At the next visit, he said he would do it.

"Here or in the hospital?"

He came out from behind his desk and held the door open. "Here."

I didn't have a chance to ask any other questions, which was fine. I didn't want to know if it would hurt or anything like that. It was going to happen.

Later, when I told Mom it was not going to be at the hospital, she said she knew. If I went to the hospital, they'd have to have a record, a lab report, about everything that happened. He could be fired for doing it without clearance. Maybe even thrown in jail.

Hospital boards! I could hear Lois saying, "With some hospitals, you have to convince them you'd kill yourself if they don't help you."

The rest is hard. I went three days later. When the nurse came for me, Mom gave me a hug. I looked back, and they stood there, Dad with his arm around Mom.

The nurse took me into a room and told me to undress. "Everything off." She handed me a white gown. "Open to the back."

Nothing warm and cozy. Just as well.

She returned and took me down a long hall to a room with a table. It had those stirrups. I hate them. The doctor and another nurse were already there. The doctor said something about a routine D and C. He handed a chart to the second nurse. "Excess bleeding coupled with irregularity," he said. The nurse who had given me the gown was standing a little away from the table. "Yeah, right!" was written all over her face. The light overhead was very white. Very bright. They put something over my face.

I woke up in a bed next to a window. Outside I could see cars on the street. People going places, on the move. Move on, move on, move on, they seemed to be saying.

Everybody does in their own way. I guess that's what I figured out. Dad was right, you can't choose for someone else.

Mom and Dad took me home, and I stayed in bed the rest of the day, Scruffy by my side. Grandma sat in her rocker next to my bed. We all slept on and off. Late in the afternoon there was a light knock on my door.

Dad. I put my finger to my lips, Grandma was dozing. He came in and closed the door behind him.

Dad doesn't seem to have trouble anymore with doors.

I hold my arm up, and the sun through the window casts a shadow. *My* shadow. Mine alone.

AUTHOR'S NOTE

Picture this. You're a teenage girl in 1956 and discover you're pregnant. You're terrified to tell your folks. In many communities, girls who get "in trouble" this way are "bad," "loose," "sluts." It's always the girl's fault. Nobody thinks anything about the guy. And then what happens when you start to show?

Chances are you'd be sent away to a home to give birth and give the baby away. Most of these places were run by the Salvation Army, Florence Crittenton Services, or various Catholic charities. Each had its own policies, but the basic plan for their unwed clients was the same: give birth, give up the baby. A shroud of secrecy covered the entire event.

Would you have any other choices? Abortion was illegal and dangerous. Many women tried it themselves, some with coat hangers, some with the techniques Jamie tries in this novel. "I considered suicide," a real-life Jamie told me. Another woman who helped her pregnant friend said, "We crept to this place in Brooklyn. Skulked along the street and watched to make sure no one saw us go in. Not shame, but fear." If you could find a medical professional, conditions could be unsterile. You'd often be given little or no anesthetic. Some hospitals would perform what they called a "therapeutic" abortion, but a whole raft of specialists had to testify that you were unfit to have a baby, or were a danger to yourself or others, et cetera.

Now picture this. You're a pregnant teenage girl in the twenty-first century. If you want an abortion, it's technically legal. But—and it's a big but—you still may not have that choice. It depends on where you live, how old you are, how far along you are, and whether you need your parents to approve the procedure. In 87 percent of the counties in the United States you won't be able to have a legal abortion, for there's no doctor who will do it. Even if you can get to a place that will give you an abortion, you may have to walk through a lineup of people who will scream that you're a "murderer."

Today women's options are becoming more limited. There are politically active groups that oppose choice. Some want to prohibit all abortions, even if a woman has been raped. There are a few individual members of these groups who are so opposed to "taking a life" (that of the unborn fetus) that they are willing to take the life—that is, murder—of the doctors who perform abortions. The first murder took place in 1993. By mid-2010 there had been eight such killings.

The U.S. Supreme Court case *Roe v. Wade* gave women a choice; it didn't force anyone to have an abortion. And pro-choice advocates want women to continue to have that choice as a matter of law, unlike Jamie in this novel. They are afraid that the increasing legal restrictions will bring back the days of "back-alley" abortions or women mutilating their own bodies because they can't get legal medical help.

But even with all of today's restrictions, there are still many more options than there were back in 1950s and 1960s. So why would a teen reader in the twenty-first century be interested in reading about a pregnant teen in 1956?

There's a famous quotation from the philosopher George Santayana: "Those who cannot remember the past are condemned to repeat it."

If we don't know what has happened, we can't appreciate our choices today and what we might lose if laws are changed. Although the historical setting is different, the pressures on young women remain the same. "Do it, baby, if you love me," and of course there continues to be rape.

Every event and choice depicted in this novel actually happened to someone. I interviewed dozens of women who went through these experiences in the 1950s and 1960s.

Their stories are powerful links to today: how do we make important decisions, what do we value, how do we understand what is happening to us? These are the same questions whether it's in the twentieth or twenty-first century. The all-important personal question is still "What do I want to do with my life?" And one way we can begin to think about that is by meeting and living with characters, both real and fictional.

ACKNOWLEDGMENTS

With much gratitude to all who told me their stories. They've informed Jamie with truths I could not otherwise have known. And with particular thanks to writer friends who read and believed: Anne, Phyllis, Liza, and Miriam. And to Jill Davis, who first listened and loved Jamie's voice, and then Andrew Karre, my editor, who with generosity and wisdom helped Jamie, and me, reach deeper.

ABOUTTHEAUTHOR

Ellen Levine is the author of many books, including *Henry's Freedom Box*, a Caldecott Honor book, and *Darkness Over Denmark*, which was a National Jewish Book Award finalist and was awarded the Trudi Birger Jerusalem International Book Fair Prize. Her book *Freedom's Children* won the Jane Addams book award and was named one of the Ten Best Children's Books of the Year by the New York Times. Levine is a woodcarver and a lapsed civil-rights lawyer, and she taught at Vermont College's Master of Fine Art in Writing for Children and Young Adults program.